Blood
Thorn

Blood

Thorn

A David Thorne Novel

Jack Lawrence

COPYRIGHT NOTICE

To my wife and kids. Thank you for believing I can do anything.

Chapter 1

Tears raced down her reddening cheeks as she became more certain of her decision. Even if she had not admitted it out loud. Not yet.

Caroline Baker had been sitting across from David Throne for the past hour in the worst condition he had seen her in since he began working with her and her husband six months before. They were both in their mid-forties and had been married since the day they both graduated college. Over two decades together. The couple's counseling seemed to be going well, but over the past three months, her husband Braden had only shown up a handful of times. When he did, he seemed dejected and unwilling to participate.

Caroline was sure that this was a sign their marriage was over and she had convinced herself that it was time to leave. David suspected that she had been fishing for permission for the past month, but that was something he would not grant. A decision like that had to be hers alone. Still, seeing her makeup smeared down her face and her eyes bulging and bloodshot from the tears, he wondered how he could in good conscious believe this man had any redeeming qualities.

"This is not how I pictured my life, David."

"Something has kept you in the marriage this long. What has kept you in the relationship up to this point?" David asked the question, but he already knew the answer. But like with any client, he was not so sure she did.

Caroline took a few long seconds to answer. David let her ponder on the question without interruption. Even when she responded, "I don't know," he said nothing. He wanted her to find her own answer; if he chimed in, she never would. At last, she responded, "When we first met, he was so caring and loving. We had imagined this great life together, you know? Both working good jobs—which we do—and then eventually kids and we would have built this life together."

Caroline wiped the tears from her face. "But now he is never there. Like, we are together, but mentally, he is not there. And when we go to the beach house, he spends more time with the guys than he does with me. We bought the house because we figured it would help us relax and make it easier to conceive. But now it seems like he doesn't care. And the chances of us conceiving are probably gone."

"Then what keeps you?"

Realizing she had not answered the question, she took a deep breath. "I'm scared to be alone and I guess a part of me still believes our storybook ending is possible."

"Now you are not as sure?"

Caroline shook her head. "No. I think I am done."

"How would you *know* if you were done?" In David's experience, very few people ever knew they were finished with a problem until they were at a point where sticking with it would hurt them more than leaving it. He was not sure Caroline had reached that point, but she seemed close. Scary close.

"I am done. I cannot keep living like this."

"So, what is your next step do you think?"

"I am speaking with a lawyer tomorrow to draw up some paperwork. I will give them to Braden this weekend."

"That is a big step. One where you sound pretty certain," David leaned in closer to Caroline to show that he was attentive to her. "How do you think he will react?"

Caroline's eyes widened and she let out a soft chuckle. "He will be pissed. But I plan on telling him somewhere public."

"Do you think he will react violently?"

"Well, I don't think he would hit me if that is what you are asking. But I don't think it will be a pleasant conversation."

David leaned back. "Well, we are almost out of time. If you need any support or want to meet after you talk with him, just let me know. We can even get the two of you in here to talk together if you want."

"Thank you for everything, David."

"I haven't done anything but listen." David stood with Caroline and walked to the door with her.

"That is more than you could ever imagine," she told him.

David opened the door and went out to the lobby of his office with her, he stopped by the receptionist's desk and reminded her again that he would be available if Caroline or Braden needed anything. Again, Caroline thanked him and scheduled to meet again one week from then with Harriet.

David returned to his office and closed the door. He was used to tough clients and seeing couples on the brink of the end. He always felt bad for them and he always did his best to allow them the space to explore their options. With Caroline, it felt different. It was as if he had failed her in some way. He was not sure why or where but his gut churned as he heard the door to the lobby open and close.

He scanned the walls of his office. They were lined with framed accolades, credentials, and awards.

A large bookcase lined the far back wall full of books on therapy models and reference guides he had not looked at in years. His oak desk sat on the left wall so he could look out the window to the right which spied on a lake. In the center of the room sat a gray chair and matching four-seat couch, and a dark oak table that matched his desk separated the two.

David had owned his practice for the past five years and it was much different now than it was when he started from a one-room office he rented in an office complex. He was well known for his work and he took deep pride in it. But as he replayed the meeting with Caroline in his mind, he felt as though he was fresh out of grad school again. Lost and unsure of himself.

There was a light knock on his door. He stepped back and opened it to allow Harriet into his office.

"Tough session?"

"The toughest I have had in a while, Mother." It had occurred to him early on that working with his mom would be an interesting balance in boundaries. Separating personal from business, and to him 'mother' seemed more professional than 'mom.' So, the title stayed.

"Well, if they were easy, they wouldn't need you." Harriet had worked most of her life as a receptionist at a hospital. As a single mother, it was hardly enough to get David through college, but she sacrificed everything she could to make sure he had opportunities she never had. Two years after she had retired David opened his practice. He was not able to pay for a secretary so Harriet offered up some of her free time. Now, five years later, she was making more than she did in any two years at the hospital and was proud of her son's accomplishments.

As he looked at her from his position, he realized, at sixty-eight, she reminded him of Mrs. Claus. She had thick glasses to aid her failing sight, her snow-white hair was permed—a style she had since he could remember—and despite it being summer, she wore a long-sleeved red shirt. Her sight was not all time had begun to take from her, either. He noticed she seemed shorter; a full foot shorter than he at six feet. But she had a warmth radiating from her that he knew the clients appreciated just as much as he did.

Having spent so much time working with David she had grown an uncanny ability to tell when a case was bothering him. He looked particularly drained by this one. "She is a smart woman, Davey. Some people just are not meant to be together."

David shook his head, still unable to shake the feeling gnawing at his gut, "It's not that. I just have a bad feeling about all of this."

"You don't think her husband will do anything crazy, do you?"

"I only met him a few times. He rarely came in. He didn't seem like the type and there is no history there, just feels off."

"Well, your six canceled, so how about you come over to my house and I'll make your favorite."

David let out a sigh, trying desperately to release the tension growing within him. "Sounds good, mom." David headed to his desk. "I will meet you there. Say, eight?"

Harriet smiled and left the office.

David spent the next twenty minutes staring blankly out of his office window. He had been a therapist long enough to know when to trust his gut, the problem was, this time he did not know what his gut was telling him. He did not think Caroline was in danger. He did not think that Braden would hurt her. And he knew that it was not his place to guide her in what she should or should not do, that was something only she could answer. Still, his gut stung from the sense that he had failed Caroline.

CHAPTER 2

A week had passed since David and Caroline's session. For the most part, he thought about their conversation less and less. Even the heavy feeling in his stomach had subsided throughout the week. However, fifteen minutes after her session was to begin, Caroline was not in the office. She had not called or e-mailed to cancel or reschedule. In the six months David had been working with Caroline and her husband—and then eventually just Caroline—she had only missed one session, and she had called two days in advance to let him know.

A shooting pain returned to his stomach as his body went cold and his heart rate picked up. He was not sure why he was having such a severe reaction to her absence, even if things had not gone well between Caroline and Braden, he had no reason to react in such a manner. David stood from his seat in the middle of the office and went to the lobby.

David looked at his mother who was just hanging up the phone. "She is not answering," Harriet said in a somber tone. Though she had given no second thoughts to Caroline's previous session, she grew concerned now.

"Cancel my next session."

"Are you okay?" Harriet began to stand from her chair but David motioned for her to remain seated.

"Not so much. I am going to call Jack."

The concern in Harriet's eyes grew. Jack Marlow was David's childhood friend. In fact, Jack was almost like a second son to her. He and David met at school when they were in the second grade and had been thick as thieves ever since. For the past five years, Jack had been a detective for the Indianapolis Metropolitan Police Department and was always David's first call when he needed to make a report for a client. Most of the time it was not something the homicide detective would deal with, but by calling Jack, David knew that it would be handled swiftly and by the best.

"It's just one session, Davey. Do you think that is really necessary? Maybe she talked with her husband and just needed time alone. Lord knows I did after my divorce."

"Normally I would agree, Mother. But Caroline would at least call. Or e-mail. It isn't like her to just ghost me on a session."

"That is true."

David reentered his office. He noticed perspiration forming on his palms as he reached for his silenced phone which rested squared in the center of a stack of papers at his desk. He scrolled through his contacts until he found Jack and made the call.

The phone rang twice before a powerful voice answered, "Davey Boy! Calling to brag about your team finally making the Final Four?"

Since they were kids David and Jack always made a wager on the NCAA tournament. David always chose Vanderbilt—now his Alma Mater—and since their betting began, Vanderbilt had only made the tournament nine times, never making it to the Final Four. Until that past March, almost three months ago. When they were not in, he would usually just choose the team holding the best record. But that was not why he was calling.

"Actually, it is a business call."

"Oh," Jack's strong voice lowered and became peaceful. A tactic he said he learned from David. "What's going on?"

"I'm not sure. I have a client who might be missing."

"What does that mean? *Might* be?"

"Well, they missed their appointment this week," before David could continue, Jack interrupted.

"That does not mean they are missing. Do you have reason to believe they are in danger?"

"If you didn't love the sound of your voice so much, you could have let me finish. They were going to inform their partner they wanted a divorce. The partner has never abused or assaulted the client, but I have had a bad feeling ever since our last meeting. This client is always fifteen minutes early and has only missed one session in six months."

"I get why you are uneasy about it, but I don't know that it constitutes police intervention, Dave. They might just be dealing with the shitstorm of asking for a divorce and your appointment got spaced."

"I don't think so, not with them."

"Do you have a release?"

David let out a sigh knowing that he did not. He technically could not give Jack any identifying information unless he *knew* Caroline was in danger because of a direct threat or she had given written consent. He had neither. David knew he could lose his license by giving Jack her information without her consent, but he felt strongly that something was wrong. To him, it was a risk worth taking.

"Yes," the lie came out easier than he expected. He was not sure if that should concern him or if it was a sign of his certainty in her danger. He would psychoanalyze that mess later. "I had her sign one when she first said she was scared of what her husband would do when she asked for the divorce."

Jack sat silent for a moment. David wondered if Jack was gauging his bull-shit meter or if he was weighing the pros and cons of believing David. Then he spoke, "Give me her name, number, and address. I will personally check in on this myself."

"Well, I didn't say it was a homicide."

"If your client is fine and just spaced your meeting, I don't think we want a record of why the police were at their house."

David smiled. He should have known Jack would hear through his lies, "Thanks, man. I owe you."

"Yeah, you do. I get off duty at eight. I will do a wellness check and meet you at the Lounge around nine."

"See you then.Thanks again, Jack."

"Don't get too happy. Your pockets are going to be empty with how many whiskeys you'll be buying tonight."

David let out a laugh and then hung up. If it turned out Caroline was okay, he would gladly spend the money on the drinks. If she was not, he would need every drop the bar held. Either way, it was an expense David did not mind spending.

⚜

The Lounge was only ten blocks from David's office. At eight-thirty he made his way through the busy downtown Indianapolis streets and into the bar. The Lounge was a modern speakeasy, promptly transporting the patron back to the roaring 20s upon entering. The walls were lined in gray stone with wooden pillars every twenty-four inches.

The lighting was dim and romantic though rarely had David ever seen anyone on a date. It was typically well-to-do men conducting business or drinking away the demons of the day. Or of their life. The mahogany bar smelled of authentic wood lined with intricate carvings of lions in mid-roar. Matching chairs lined the bar laced in plush leather, the aroma of the leather mixed perfectly with the booze and mahogany.

A half dozen four-person tables were throughout the speakeasy, each matching the bar in detail and quality. Two other larger tables sat on the right and left ends of the room, with long pew-style seats on either side. David found a table in the corner where others would be less likely to hear a conversation between him and Jack, he then stuck a finger in the air beckoning the waiter.

A few moments later a man in his thirties arrived. He was so slender the black vest around his chest sagged and his matching black pants looked baggy. Even his bow tie could not shrink enough to sit snug at his throat.

"What can I get for you, sir?" The young man's voice matched his frail appearance.

"I'll take two Jack Daniel's on the rocks."

"Very well, sir."

The waiter was gone before David could say another word. As he waited for Jack, he noticed his leg bouncing uncontrollably under the table. He also noticed that he was holding his breath as he waited for Jack to enter the bar.

CHAPTER 3

While sipping on his second drink David saw Jack enter the bar. His shirt was unbuttoned and his hair was slicked back. Jack looked as though he were stuck in the role of some 1980s villain, even though he was a cop and even though he was born at the tail end of the 80s. He moved easily through the bar toward David. David was impressed at his ability to find a target even in a dimly lit room that was not as empty as it had been even fifteen minutes previous.

Jack sat down heavily and took a swig from his warming glass.

"So?"

"So, what?" The bourbon deepened Jack's voice a whole octave.

"Did you find out anything?"

Jack leaned back in his seat and David could not tell if he had and was merely soaking in the view before his boastful reveal, or if he had found nothing and was mentally preparing for David to head off toward a catastrophic theory.

"I called her work and she did not show up today and did not call. She has not been in or called in for the past three days. Which is kind of lucky for you because her office called in a wellness check so you dodged that bullet in your ass. I also went by her house, both she and her husband's cars were in the garage." He took another sip of his whiskey before continuing.

"When the cops doing the check went in, they did notice some clothes looked to be missing and so were their wallets and toiletries."

"That's odd. If they were in a hurry to get out why bother with toiletries?"

"Maybe they weren't in a hurry. Maybe your client broke the news about a divorce, they had a heart-to-heart, and decided they needed some time away to rekindle the old flame."

David contemplated this. Caroline was a romantic and Braden had shown glints of a Casanova persona in the past. "It just isn't like her to miss a session and not cancel. But to miss three days of work and not say anything? That is absolutely out of character for her."

Jack downed his glass and waved it in the air to signal the waiter for another. He took a deep breath, "Lord help me. Is there anywhere special they may have gone? I can do some digging and see if they wound up there."

David thought for a moment replaying their six months of conversation in his mind. Then, "Yes. They have a house in Havana."

Havana was the Indiana equivalent of the Hamptons in New York. It was a small town within a small town where only the rich or connected vacationed. The ultra-rich owned property within its gated confines. It sat just southwest of Michigan City in northern Indiana, nestled tightly to Lake Michigan. The town allowed visitors to rent a few beach homes which were used specifically for the purpose of renting. But the people who visited were just on the outskirts of the fortune of the homeowners and for a weekend could pull off belonging there.

"Jesus Christ," Jack growled. "I can't help you there, buddy."

"What do you mean?"

"I mean that's like its own fucking country. They have a police force of maybe fifteen officers. The Mayor and the Chief both forbid outside interference. They run their ship that way. I can't call up there and ask questions without a court's backing."

"Then I will do it."

"What do you mean, 'you will do it'?"

"I mean I will go up there and stay until I get some answers."

The waiter slid Jack's new glass onto the table and swiped the old one away in what looked like one fluid motion. Jack took a swig while he waited for the man in the oversized black vest to vanish. "That's not the type of place you just go askin' questions, Davey. You'll end up in jail, with a fine, or tossed out on the highway somewhere. And do not forget they will not look the other way with you breaking confidentiality. They'll use that against you to keep you out of their business."

"You make it sound like the mob. It is a small town of uptight rich people. I have spent my fair share of time with them."

"No," Jack said shaking his head. "You work for some of them. But their kind of money could buy a hundred of those prissy sports cars you got out there."

"First off," David said with a grin, "as I recall, you couldn't wait to borrow the Jaguar when you had that date a few months ago."

"A lot of good it did, she didn't even show up."

"Look, I can go up for a few days and just check out their house. Bring them up in casual conversation to see if anyone has seen them. If they have and they are fine I will come right back. If they haven't then I will let you guide my next play."

Jack's discomfort was palatable but David knew Jack would back him on it. Jack had not ever tried to stop David from making a stupid decision. Specifically, when Jack knew that David was not going to take no for an answer anyhow.

"You got three days to figure something out or I am coming up there to drag your ass back here myself. Got that?"

"Yeah. I got it."

David dropped a one-hundred-dollar bill on the table to cover the drinks and the tip and stood to leave.

"Hey," Jack said. "Mind if I borrow the Jag tomorrow. Got a date." He was not so much asking as he was making David aware. "You do owe me after all."

David shook his head with a grin, "Sure thing, pal."

CHAPTER 4

David sat outside of his apartment for a long time after he arrived home. He had spent a few minutes on his navigation application estimating how long it would take him to get to Havana, booking a rental for a week, and trying to formulate a reason for him to be there. Jack was known for being paranoid but David had not felt right since Caroline left his office the week before. Perhaps he would benefit from being a little paranoid as well. Especially with how Jack described Havana.

David entered the building where a concierge, Samuel, was waiting. Samuel welcomed David with a warming smile and a subtle nod. Samuel was about the same age as David but doubled his size. His smile wrapped around his entire face in an almost villainous sort of way, but somehow David had come to look forward to the smile. Particularly on the harder days and this was one such day.

"Hello, Mr. Thorne. Can I get you anything this evening?"

"No thank you, Sam. How is everything going on your front?"

"Oh, I cannot complain Mr. Thorne. I have a wife who loves me, a warm home, and a job I enjoy."

David smiled at his words. "That is a beautiful way of looking at life, Sam. If only more people could see it that way."

"Indeed, Mr. Thorne."

"Well, goodnight, Sam."

"Goodnight.

David rode the elevator to the fifteenth floor where his penthouse rested. Samuel's words played in his mind. *I have a wife who loves me, a warm home, and a job I enjoy.* Again, David thought how much better the world would be if everyone adopted such an outline. How much easier his job would be if they assumed such a truth. How much better his own life might be if he accepted such simplicities as a measure of happiness.

At thirty-five he was financially well, lived in a penthouse, drove a Jaguar, and had the most exclusive clients in the state, willing to pay $250 an hour out of pocket, for just an hour of his time each week. He saw thirty clients a week, had limited overhead, did a few speaking engagements a year, and had written two best-selling self-help books. Financially, he could not ask for more.

Still, his home would be empty when he walked through the door. He had his share of romantic inquiries but he always said he was waiting for the "right time." As if any time would be *right*. In truth, he was not sure why he had not committed to anyone, but before he could sink deeper into his self-pity the elevator door opened to his floor.

He went to the right and slid his key into the first door he came to. It was already unlocked. David's heart began to pick up the pace and warm perspiration started at his palms and then arrived quickly at his back and then his scalp. His suit jacket suddenly seemed to tighten around him.

There was no reason for his door to be unlocked. David took a deep breath and shook it off. He accused the fine whiskey and Jack's paranoia of polluting his logical thinking. The probability of someone breaking into his apartment was almost zero. The people who lived in the building had everything he had, most had better versions of it. Anyone who might sneak into the building to rob someone would stand out like black smoke to a clear sky. He took another deep breath and steeled himself before pushing the door open.

Once inside he was relieved to see he was alone. The living room light was lit, dimly as he had left it. Nothing jumped out to him as being out of place and his laptop still sat open on the island. Then he heard a soft squeak.

His eyes followed the sound to the hall on his right which led to a stairway leading to his second bedroom, which he used as an office, as well as his own bedroom. Downstairs was the guest bathroom. A shadow stood in the hall and began walking towards him. David's voice was frozen in his throat and his muscles locked in place.

Then the figure emerged from the dark hallway into the small halo of light provided by the lamp in the living room.

"Can't say 'hi' to your mother anymore?" Harriet stood at the hall's entrance with her hands fisted to her hips. She took in his face and then her pretend snarl turned to a look of concern, "Are you okay?!"

"You scared the hell out of me! What are you doing here?"

"I came to check on you, what happened to you?"

David dropped his briefcase to the floor and let out a hard exhale. He rubbed his hand over his face vigorously wiping away the feeling of cowardice. He had been scared nearly shitless by a sixty-eight-year-old woman half his height. If Jack could see him now.

"I am fine, Mother. No need to check in on me."

"That's not the way I hear it," she said as she walked closer to her son. She stopped at the island and pulled a bottle of wine from the wine case built into it.

"What do you mean?" David met her at the island, grabbing two glasses from overhead.

"Jack called me."

"Snitch."

"He's worried."

"About what?" David poured the wine from the bottle his mother had just opened, not even taking the time to see which she had chosen. It was a deep red and he could not wait for it to push his nerves back down.

"You."

"How is that?" David slid his mother her glass and took a slow drink from his own. It was a sweet wine with a hint of something sharp.

"He said you are going to Havana to look for Caroline?"

"Yeah."

"And that doesn't seem off to you?"

David knew it sounded crazy. No therapist should insert themselves into a client's life. Especially when the client does not show up to just one session. He knew the right thing to do would be to call Caroline a couple of times and if she did not show up for the next session, report it to the police and allow them to do their job. This was different. He felt a sense of guilt with her that he had not felt since he was an intern.

24

"I could see how to someone else it might. To me, it does not."

"You don't know that anything terrible has even happened."

"No, I don't." David finished his glass in one sharp swig. Something he never allowed himself to do on a normal occasion. Wine was to be enjoyed, not chugged. "But I told her that everything would be fine. If it is not fine then that is on me."

"No, it is on whoever hurt her. Assuming anything has happened at all. Jack said he thought Caroline and her husband were probably in Havana patching things up."

"And I hope he's right, in which case it will be a quick trip."

"And if he isn't? What can you do that the police cannot?"

David pondered the question for a moment, then poured himself another glass. "Sleep at night."

Harriet leaned over and hugged her son.

The figure watched them from outside. He stood in the woods shielded behind the cover of trees. He could see them, but they could not see him. Amateurs leave the lights on in the house where anyone from the outside could see their every move.

He could tell they were arguing and he laughed to himself imagining what they were saying to each other.

They should have never come back here, but they were dumb enough to leave themselves exposed in the house so why not be dumb enough to come back? The figure would take care of that, though. They would be punished for their sins, the figure standing in as judge, jury, and hopefully, executioner.

The figure slid a hand down the right side and felt the cold steel of the gun at the hip. Another bloodthirsty smile rounded the figure's face.

CHAPTER 5

Two days later David had his duffle bag of clothing and toiletries resting in his back seat. He sat in the driver's seat now doubting his decision to go looking for Caroline and her husband. Thoughts of losing his licensure, losing a client, and his name being tarnished by this one decision to pry on a client's personal life without just reason. He could lose his practice, his home, his car, and his entire lifestyle hung in the balance because of this one decision. If the board found out that he had broken confidentiality and had gone on a one-man crusade to find a missing client—who was not even legally missing—and they would rain down judicial fury. He wished his old mentor Dr. Utek was still alive.

Dr. Utek had been a family therapist longer than David had been alive when they met in David's second year of grad school. Dr. Utek had been assigned to be David's supervisor when he entered practicum and internship, meaning once a week for an hour they would meet and talk about David's cases. David learned the ins and outs of how to read between the lines—reading people's actions over their words, the context over the content—and he learned how to ask the questions that made people

27

talk. When David graduated and passed his exam it was Dr. Utek who supervised him for the following two years. The man had become David's mentor, but more closely, the father he had not been able to know.

Dr. Utek would ask David, "What makes her different than anyone else? What about this case strikes you so deeply? Who does she remind you of?"

David shook the thought away. Even in his mind, he did not want to dwell on the questions he knew he should be asking himself. He did know, however, that if he did not at least know Caroline was safe, he could not live with himself. To know that he had done nothing to help her when she put so much confidence in him. Deep down, of course, he knew that anything that had happened to her was not caused by him. Still, the guilt reared itself each time he doubted his actions.

He began to wonder where this doubt was the night before when he had made the hasty decision to sneak into Caroline's home, half desperate to find her there and half desperate to not be swarmed by an army of officers, guns drawn and lasers tracing his chest. The home was nestled in Meridian Hills, the wealthiest community in Indianapolis. It a straight drive north from his apartment. Finding the community was easy. Finding the home was the challenge. Meridian Hills was its own town, with an apartment complex, a golf course, and mansions scattered throughout. Each one with security cameras monitoring the roads.

It had been late—nearly one in the morning—and no one would logically be out that late on a Thursday who was not looking for trouble. David parked two blocks away in the mostly vacant parking lot of a nearby Stop-Go. When he neared the brick wall that lined the community, he tucked his body close, praying that his clearly odd behavior would go unnoticed—since the roads were desolate his prayers were easily answered. The wall only stood about five feet, and there was a flash of pride when he was able to climb it on his first go.

Once over the gate, he ran to his right where a patch of woods would serve as his cover. He knew from the maps online that he could follow the tree line past two houses until he reached Caroline's. Nothing about navigating the neighborhood made sense to David. The golf course and clubhouse were at the front of the community and the mansions were scattered, rather than symmetrically placed.

The house David was looking for was not outwardly impressive, David thought, for all the to-dos the neighborhood put on. It stood two stories. The bottom half was orange-colored brick while the top had light siding. There seemed to be more windows than space, though none of them looked out of place.

David crept around to the rear of the house and arrived at a wooden staircase that led to a deck on the second level. He looked around and felt putting himself higher up somehow made him more of a target, so he ducked into the protection of the shadows provided by the deck overhead. There was a single glass door—with two other large panes on either side—which he was able to use to peer into the house.

The house was dark, but small accent lights allowed just enough vision to show the room was empty. It looked like no one had been in there for days. He reached for the knob of the door expecting to be stopped by a locked handle, he could say he gave it a shot and go home. But the door was not locked and it did open.

The inside did not mirror the boring, unexcited exterior. The inside resembled a palace, pristine and pure. The unblemished walls were a sparkling white which, even in the near blackness, reflected the small bits of accent lights enough to allow David to navigate without much interference. The furniture all rested in the perfect geometric position to fill voids in the room but not appear crowded, and they too appeared to be unspoiled. The marble floor was white too, but not as pure as the walls, which, David imagined, provided the perfect contrast to the limpidness of the walls.

David stood still in the middle of the room for a few minutes. Quiet. Just listening. Not a single sound came from the floor above or from the floor he was on. There was a double staircase to his right which began in the living room, lead to a small landing, then flipped back around to the second floor. David moved watchfully to the stairs and was relieved to find carpet on the stairs. He was not sure exactly why he was relieved, but he felt it.

He slid his shoes off so as not to track mud on the spotless gray carpet. Each step was watchful and delicate as if one misstep and he would fall through to an abyss without escape. Once up the stairs—a process that took far longer than it should—he again stood in silence. Listening. When he still heard nothing, he went door to door, slowly opening them just enough to put his ear to the crack, each time hoping to catch the exhale of a sleeping occupant. Or the rustle of a tossing dreamer. But each room remained silent and dead.

Once he had checked each room, he went back and opened the doors a little further to glance inside. Only one room caught his attention—both for being least likely of being caught and for what it might contain—which was an office. David was sure to not turn on a light, he did not want to draw more attention to the house, not even from the animals roaming the woods beyond the window he stood in front of.

David leaned in close to the desk to aid his sight in the darkness. He found a calendar with the past week being vacant, void of even so much as a phone call. He flipped through the drawers gingerly, but nothing stuck out to him. On the far end of the desk was a picture that he only glanced at, at first. Then he looked at it again, closer, more mindful, with purpose. It was another house, a house quite a bit smaller than the one he stood in, but the exterior resembled the type of mansion he had assumed this one would be.

He knew it was their Havana house. At least now he would know which one was theirs when he arrived. He pulled his phone from his pocket and put the framed photo on the floor, turning his back to the window in hope that his flash would be blocked from the outside world. As if his frame were big enough to prevent a shred of light from escaping the large windows that ran the length of the wall. Once he had the picture he returned the frame to the desk, rearranged it four times, then twice more, and then left.

An hour before David got into his car that morning, Jack called, his voice more graveled and horse than normal. He told David that the police had contacted someone from Braden's office—no name was given, Jack was better at following protocol than David, apparently—and Braden had informed them he would be out of town for a few days. The unnamed person had also spoken with Caroline because she and his wife were friends. As far as the police were concerned the mystery had been solved and their job was done.

David still did not feel right, though. Something tugged at him that, this whole scenario was far too out of character for Caroline. Even though he guessed he really did not know the woman all that well. His job had taught him one thing, people are, at the core, who they are. There are things they can fake to boost appearances and gain the acceptance of others, but things like basic courtesy were not among them. That, one way or another, always came to light if it were being faked. Caroline's punctuality, devotion to her work, and ensuring she canceled her one missed session long before the required twenty-four hours was not a way of keeping appearances. That was her to the core. Even if she had not notified David, she would miss their appointment and would be going out of town, she would have, without doubt, told her work.

Finally, David commanded his mind to stop wondering all the what-ifs. He forced it to stop. He turned on his car, put it into gear, and after one more, "Are you sure," he pulled away from his parking spot.

CHAPTER 6

David planned to take I-65 north and then cut over east on I-94. In all the trip was estimated to take him three hours. But David had made the trip several times over the years—to Chicago negating the route east he would be taking this trip—for conferences and seminars. He never looked forward to it. Most of his trip north would be a battle of consciousness and forcing himself to keep from sleeping at the wheel. The long roads through mostly country state roads were almost hypnotic and with no visual stimulus, made the eyelids grow heavy.

Most of the trip heading north, until he reached Crown Point, would be all farm. Over the past decade or so, many farmers had caved to the pressures of energy companies and big paydays, selling chunks of their land to windmill companies. The farmland—boring on its own—was not as boring and hideous as it was when littered with hundreds of white windmills, the vast majority of which never seemed to move. The days of seeing old barns and farmhouses with charm and character, full of stories from the generations of families inhabiting them were long gone.

He and his mother used to travel to Chicago every year to visit her family. They had all passed or moved over the years. Now his only trips to Chicago were alone and to a conference. But when they would travel, his mother would pick out a farm or a barn and they would create the entire history of the building in their minds. They would talk about the families that had lived within the walls, the products they farmed, and how they spent their Sunday afternoons. On occasion, though rare, he still did this himself when he would pass by an interesting enough building. He wondered how many cars passing the old structures appreciated the history within them as much as he had grown to. He guessed very few.

During his conversation with Jack a few hours before he departed, Jack had asked if David took the time to look at Havana on Google Maps. He had not. When he did, he garnished a newfound appreciation for Jack's reluctance for David to go. The entire area of the map where Havana should have been was blurred out. A square patch of fuzzy screen where nothing distinguishable could be found, and when zoomed in on, the fuzzy screen gave way to blackness.

David thought it was his app, his phone, or maybe even his connection. But as he swiped from one town, one city, one state to the next, Havana was the only location with this blocking feature.

Normally, he might not have thought much about it. But given his instructions for checking into his rental home, it grew even more bizarre. Though he did not share this with Jack, knowing that the man's paranoia would cause him to conduct a 4 a.m. raid on David's apartment and detain him until he came to his senses.

The woman David spoke to gave him an address. Not to a house—of course not—but to a shipping store four miles outside of Havana. It was a small local business that shipped packages from all the major carriers but also had personal mailboxes. The woman told him he had to arrive before 6 p.m. and give the worker his last name and mention the box number—three-twenty-three—and he would be given an envelope. Inside, he would find the key to the house, the gate combination to get into Havana, and detailed instructions on not just finding Havana, but how to navigate once inside the gates.

David wondered how a town so secretive could even allow rentals. It sounded more like a third-world dictatorship masquerading within the country than a community for the rich. Havana owned five miles of beach on Lake Michigan, overreaching into the Indiana Dunes State Park, in which no person without the permission of Havana would be permitted to step foot. By looking at the blurred spot on his map, David guessed Havana took up enough land to fit a small city of ten thousand, yet less than thirty people owned property within the gated walls.

Suddenly, David wondered, what did Caroline and Braden do that required them to live within such protected environments. Their everyday home was in a gated community, but even their vacation home was walled in, ensuring whatever they wanted out, stayed that way. David knew Caroline worked a menial job—at least in terms of needing such security—as a market designer. She made good money, but David had hired his share of marketing firms. Even the worst designer would not be so bad to cause someone to want to hunt them down.

He could not recall—not entirely anyway—what Braden did. He was a lawyer of some sort. But David knew plenty of lawyers from all areas of law, and not one of them felt the need to go to such extreme measures to keep their lives private. He was also relatively certain that Braden was not a partner or owner in a firm, which would almost certainly be required for the fortune this couple had. David was a cash-only therapist and he charged more than most people's cellphone bill. Their home in Meridian Hills was close to a million based on his research, and while he did not know the income bracket required to own a home in Havana, he guessed it would be more money than he would see in two lifetimes.

CHAPTER 7

Three and a half hours after leaving his parking spot, David arrived at the Ship-It station, just as he had been instructed by the feminine voice on the phone forty-eight hours before. The woman sounded young, her prim yet haughty tone fit both her voice's age and the town she worked in. David imagined a twenty-something girl in a white blouse and beach blond hair. Her nails were artistically styled and brought to a point just beyond the tip of her finger's end. Bright red lipstick lined her lips and her green eyes rolled as she grilled David over the phone.

"What will you be doing while in Havana? How long will you be staying? Do you know anyone in Havana? How long have you been with your employer?"

The interrogation was almost as grueling as the process required to become a therapist. She even made sure to remind him of the cost of what his seven nights would be—four times—and reminded him that photographs were only allowed in certain areas—never with people outside of his party—and if that rule were broken there would be fines. He had been reminded of a video he had watched about North Korea and he shivered at the thought of it.

David emerged from his car, the heat of the day at its peak now that it was one in the afternoon. June, he knew, was not going to be as hot as it would get that summer. Still, the humidity and heat met his flesh and caused the perspiration to begin immediately. Fortunately, the next few days were supposed to be mild in terms of humidity, which is where the real misery was anyway. He stretched his arms above his head, extending his entire body six inches as he did. He felt his contracted muscles release in ecstasy as the knots untied and the fibers all released from one another.

David walked to the Ship-It but was cautious to not expend too much energy. He did not want to arrive at the gates of Havana drenched in sweat, fearing they would shoo him away on the spot. Undoubtedly with a police escort.

The cool AC hit his flesh as soon as he opened the door and an involuntary sigh of relief left his lips. He shivered as the coolness washed over him, nearly freezing his sweat as it touched, which he was thankful for.

"How can I help ya?" The voice was high like a mouse chirping from across the room.

David shook himself from his relief and for the first time examined his surroundings. The store was bright, which was unfortunate. It showcased the organized chaos in a way that was both unflattering and disorienting. Nothing seemed to make sense. Boxes were stacked indicating the various sizes they had in stock, and banners with their services were placed randomly on the offensive orange walls—a color that reminded David of a decaying tangerine. Two large printers sat on either side of the building, neither fitting their assigned location and appearing to have just been thrust into wherever they could fit best.

On the back wall was an array of small golden mailboxes which looked as though their best days were several decades behind them. The owner of the screeching voice was a short balding man who stood lazily behind a squared hole in the wall. The man was short enough to resemble a small child looking over a counter waiting for his dad to complete a transaction so he could hold the receipt.

David made his way to the counter and noticed the man was not standing, he was sitting. He was a round man and the way his head rested on top, he resembled a snowman. He wore narrow glasses which magnified his brown eyes. David recognized the eyes. The eyes of a man full of sorrow and void of hope. His voice and attitude verified David's hunch.

"What. Can. I. Do. For. You?" The man asked again, this time annunciating each word in an agitated voice.

"My name is Thorne, box…"

Suddenly, the man's hopeless eyes lit up and his lethargic body moved with an impressive athleticism David had not expected. The man dashed from his seat and vanished behind a wall to the left—when he stood the man was quite tall. Taller than David at six feet, and his rounded frame trimmed twenty pounds.

Seconds later the man returned with a white envelope, his eyes wide and his jaw agape. He handed David the envelope, his eyes glued to David, curious. On the front of the envelope was just one word: Thorne. Inside he found the key, the square sticky note with the gate code, and two pages of instructions on how to get to the house.

"So, you're staying in Havana, huh?" The life that came to this man over such a small thing as an envelope nearly made David chuckle, but he bit his bottom lip and swallowed hard, pushing it back.

"Yes, for a few days. You ever been?"

"Oh, no! I could never afford it working in this shit-hole."

"Do you know much about it?" David tucked the envelope and its contents into his front right pocket, keeping his hand over the envelope to ensure nothing escaped.

"Not really. I remember when they were building it, everyone thought it was going to be some sort of military base."

"Really? Why is that?"

"Cause, it is right on the lake. It is freaking massive. The whole damn thing is gated in. Plus, it butts up to the park, so you know, government land and all that."

"Ever meet anyone from Havana?"

The man rolled his eyes and smirked, "Shit no. They are too good to come here. Havana has a private carrier they all use and any printing jobs they need they probably do at home. And best believe they wouldn't be caught dead in this town for anything else." The man's dialog rambled on like a string of words, both excited and insulted. "You're the first person who has rented a house out there in months."

"Not many visitors, huh?"

"I hear they are pretty selective about who they let visit?" The man was asking rather than telling.

"They certainly are."

"So, what do you do? How did you get in?" He asked in a, *you think you're better than me?* tone.

"I know someone who has a house there. I am a therapist also, so I assume my line of work isn't threatening."

"How does that make you feel?"

David liked this guy. He made a mental note to come back and offer to buy him a beer when this was all over with.

⁂

Once David was sure that the man had little more else to offer but decent conversation, he left. His hand still cradled the envelope in his pocket until he got into his Jaguar and placed it into his center dash. For the first time since arriving, he scanned the town. He wondered why people would build a town such as Havana here.

It did not fit.

The town was run down, holding all the problems of Chicago without the money. Without the glamour. There were no skyrises or fancy theaters, no fine dining. Only remnants of buildings suggesting that at one time, a time probably more recent than David would have guessed, the town held real life. Now, though, all that remained were the leftovers. Broken down cars—or at least based on appearance seemed broken down—lined the streets. People in worn clothes walked the streets, some of them

44

already drunk by late afternoon. Some of them, he knew, were probably high.

On the other side of the lake, on a clear day, not like then, you could see the towering buildings of Chicago. Almost as if it were sticking its tongue out and waiving its fingers on either side of its head at the town. Saying, "Take our garbage but not our riches." Then David had a thought.

Perhaps that was why Havana was built. An opportunity for the rich to sit higher on their pedestals, to live a protected and secluded life, while just inches from their gate the peasants graveled. Wishing they could be part of their world. To just, for one day, taste the sweetness a fat bank account provided.

David knew better. He had been raised by a single mother for most of his childhood. They were not poor, but just barely. The alimony had covered most of the bills and his mom saved what was left. They could vacation, but did so on the cheap. David had a car on his sixteenth birthday, but only because he had been saving for one since he was thirteen. Now, here he sat amid the downtrodden in a Jaguar only two years old.

Back home he lived in a luxury skyrise, his office lease was as much as some people's rent. He went to plays and ate at some of the finest restaurants cities had to offer. He could vacation most anywhere—as he proved to himself now—without having to budget too long. Part of it was living in the Midwest, where taxes were much lower than on the coasts and other big cities. Still, he had lived on both sides of the fence.

But David learned long ago that he could not save the world. In the grand scheme of things, he was as powerless as the man stumbling off the curb twenty yards in front of him. He was as powerless as the small town had been when the businesses left, taking with it the hope. He found he could only help those who asked for it, and they could save themselves. It had to be a collective.

His thoughts then turned to Caroline. Why then, was he here? Why had he driven three hours with no proof of any harm being done to this woman, just to make sure she was all right? Whom was he trying to save? Her? Himself? He could not answer that. He supposed he couldn't until he found her.

CHAPTER 8

David's hand was sweaty as he began entering his code. He felt like a covert spy sneaking behind enemy lines, not daring to look at cameras, not daring to make any sudden movements, making himself as invisible as he could. But it was a delicate balance. He had to show he belonged among the inhabitants of Havana if he were to successfully infiltrate the fortress, yet he also had to go unnoticed and not draw attention to himself.

Once David entered the last digit of the code, the heavy metal gate, coated in a deep black paint, shook. Even the gate questioned David's intentions, trying to decide if David was a threat to the way of life laying beyond it. Or, if he were a harmless visitor wanting to brag to his friends that he stayed in the reclusive Havana community. As if the gate decided David was harmless it lifted into the sky, towering over his car like a skyscraper from the city more so than just a simple gate.

David drove across the threshold suddenly engulfed by large red maples and flowering dogwoods. The whites, reds, and light pinks of the maples added splashes of variance to the deep sea of crimson surrounding him. The unfathomable beauty

47

and richness of the colors stole his eyes from the road. Though the tallest of the trees stood only seven feet, it seemed like he had been swallowed whole by the trees, as if they wrapped around him threatening to never let go. As his eyes scanned the waves of vibrant color, he did not care if they ever did.

Once he broke through the threshold of the trees, he pulled his car over to the side of the road. He retrieved the paper with the typed instructions on how to navigate the town-within-a-town toward his rental. The notes took an entire page, David scanned the scenery before him and he saw houses spread around, an area that resembled the center of a town, but he could not be sure due to distance. He noticed the road he was on branched off into three directions just a few hundred yards ahead, and he began to realize how easily one might become lost in Havana.

The paper instructed him to take the first right, then the second left, another right, and then a sharp left which would take him down to the western part of the community. His rental would be the two-story white house with blue shutters—the only house on the street with a widow's tower. A nice touch, he thought.

David drove slower than he had since his first day in driver's ed twenty years ago. Navigating the road with too much caution, ensuring he would not make a wrong turn. Once he made the final sharp left turn—wondering why the instructions navigated him through two rights instead of left at the beginning— he felt his hands loosen on the wheel and the tension in his neck released. He was not sure how far he was from his rental, but he began taking in the sights around him.

Houses were spaced out every one-hundred yards or so. Each house was separated by a line of northern hemlock trees creating a natural-looking property divider. However, the trees looked out of place in the sand that made up the yards. Some homes had grass put in, but most seemed to go for the beach vibe. Between some houses he could see out to Lake Michigan, other houses had their views blocked by dunes, at least their first floor, the second story of the homes with blocked views would be unobscured, he thought.

David passed eight houses before coming to the final house on the road. A white, two-story home with deep blue shutters matching the vibrance of the lake behind, and the widow's tower. The driveway was sealed concrete and his yard was covered in grass. However, when he parked, he realized the grass was turf. To the left of the house was nothing but an open beach and sand. He felt like he had left Indiana and entered Florida.

He got out of the car and stood beside it, admiring the house before him. It looked cozy.

Homey. Welcoming. He could see himself having a very relaxing vacation there, taking a break from the hecticness of his work and the turmoil he carried for his clients. But that would have to come another time, right now, he was there for work.

David pulled his phone from his pocket and scrolled through his phonebook, stopping at his mother's name, and hitting the call button. She answered on the second ring.

"Did you get there safe?"

"Yes."

"What is it like?"

"It is beautiful, as you would suspect. I will send some pictures."

"You better," she said in a tone only mothers could produce.

"Any calls or e-mails I need to take care of?"

David could hear his mother flipping through some papers. He had taught her—and retaught her at least twice a week—how to use the computer for notes, scheduling, and everything in between. But Harriet was old school, she liked keeping everything on paper so that she knew where to find it. If the computer crashed, she wanted to know that her work would be unscathed. She knew how to work the e-mail, and to her, that was more than enough. David had mused with her that she would rather clients send stamped envelopes over e-mails.

After a few moments of searching, she found whatever it was she had been looking for. "You had three new clients reach out. I put them on the schedule for two weeks out and e-mailed them the paperwork.

"You had one client; Brad Griffith says he needs to go to Europe for business and will call when he gets back. Daryl McKnight and his wife Katrina say they need to meet for an emergency meeting. If it cannot wait until next week, I gave them your referrals."

David took a deep breath. He loved working for himself and having his private practice. It was his pride and joy. The thing which claimed most of his time and thoughts and even his sleep. But it was times like this he was reminded of the darker part of it. How quickly—only one day away—things can grow out of hand. Three new clients would have to wait two weeks to see him, and a couple in distress now had to meet with someone they did not know or trust in his absence. But David knew all too well the impact burnout could have on someone. He had experienced its wrath firsthand, and while he was not on vacation, he had to remind himself that he was not at the office either. Harriet could handle whatever was thrown their way, and in the end, even if one or two clients were pissed off he was out and they left, he was in no shortage of people seeking his services.

"Okay," he said, "I will call you again tomorrow to check in. If anything major happens let me know."

"And you do the same on your end."

David knew what she meant. If he found Caroline, let her know! "Will do."

CHAPTER 9

David returned to his car after taking his single bag into the house. He did not bother taking a tour of the house outside of the fragments he saw searching for the garage and opening the door. His mind was too occupied with thoughts of how he would search for Caroline without being too suspicious. He knew the people who owned real estate in Havana would not appreciate someone snooping around, particularly someone who had no business being there in the first place.

He was getting ready to park his Jaguar in the garage when he heard the soft hum of an electric engine, which was easily drowned out by a gravelly voice, one that sounded as if a fist full of rocks had been jammed into the throat. "Hey!"

David froze. He turned slowly toward the sound. An older man, in his mid-fifties or so, came stomping up the driveway, a four-seat golf cart behind him. The man wore khakis, deck shoes, and an obnoxious Hawaiian shirt that was unbuttoned showing a forest of white chest hairs to the world. The man's hair matched the whiteness on his chest but blew wildly in the wind. David assumed in his real-life the man probably styled the hair to hide the patches of scalp sneaking through the snowy hair. But at the lake house, who cared?

Though the man was stomping he did not appear aggressive. He wore a wide smile flashing teeth whiter than the frizzled hair on his head. Then David noticed the glass of what he guessed to be a bourbon that the man touted around in his right hand.

"How are ya, neighbor?"

David reached to meet the man's now extended hand. "Good just got here," David told him. "Neighbor, huh? Where do you live?"

"One-hundred yards yonder," the man said pointing with his glass to his right. "Name is Dr. Neil Ogletree. Dr. Neil, Dr. O, or if we become friends, Doc."

David smiled, "Nice to meet you, Dr. Neil. I am David Thorne, not truly a neighbor. I rented the house for a few days."

The man lowered his head, keeping his eyes fixed on David. An investigative look of uncertainty sat on his face. As if the man doubted each word David spoke. Then, his eyes lit and a smile crashed into his face, his expression turned from skepticism to excitement. "David Thorne! I thought I recognized you, you son-of-a-bitch!" Dr. Neil shook his hand again, with more vigor this time.

"I heard your talk on family relationships and dynamics and how it influences pathology." Dr. Neil took a proud swig from his glass. David was impressed with the man's ability to recall his talk while being half drunk.

"Oh," David said, never once considering that someone from Havana may recognize him from his work or one of his speaking engagements. "Psychotherapist?"

"Oh, hell no!" Dr. Neil said with a bellowed laugh. "I don't like people enough. I am a surgeon." Dr. Neil took another, shorter, sip and his prideful glow seemed to somehow brighten. "Actually," he said, "I was a surgeon. Retired earlier this year. Now I just sit on my ass and drink. Life's finest adventure." Dr. Neil raised his glass to a solo toast.

"How long have you lived in Havana?"

"Had a house here about four years. Was an easy weekend trip and Chicago being close enough I could go back if needed. Been living here full time with the Misses since March."

David shook, "Wow! Brave man to be staying here in the winter."

Dr. Neil shrugged. "Chicago, my boy. We are well and good used to it. Considered Florida, but that is for old folks, and I got too much life left to be old."

Dr. Neil finished his glass. "Know anyone from Havana or just thought it would be a good story to tell?"

David weighed his options. He obviously would not tell Dr. Neil how he knew Caroline and Braden, but he pondered whether he should tell him he knew them at all. If they were here and the good doctor mentioned something to them, that could be a problem. If the half-drunken man began asking too many questions, that could be a problem. In the end, he decided at least mentioning their name might give credence to himself, though he was not sure how. "I know the Baker's. Caroline's firm helped me with some promotional work for one of my lectures." Only a mild lie. The firm had helped him, but it was two years before Caroline scheduled their first session.

"Good people!" Dr. Neil's eyes raised to the right, briefly lost in memory somewhere. "Come to think of it, I haven't seen them around recently. Couple weeks at least."

"Is that odd," David tried to sound nonchalant. As if he were simply being cordial in asking more about the man's concern.

"Well, not particularly, I suppose. Usually, they are up this way at least once every two weeks. So, them not coming for three weeks or so isn't too strange, but isn't too regular either."

David shrugged, trying to keep his façade of indifference going. "Well, maybe next week."

"Yeah," Dr. Neil said taking another sip from his empty glass. The melted ice seemed to fool the doctor into believing there was just enough left for him to say a few more words before retreating for more.

"Say, old boy, I am having a little soiree tomorrow night. Why don't you swing by?"

"Oh, I wouldn't want to impose!" David said. In truth, he wanted to lay low and be seen by as few people as possible. Particularly Caroline and Braden, in case they somehow managed to make the party. He came to ensure they were safe and well, not to speak with them.

"No imposition at all! Seven tomorrow night. Stay an hour, stay all night."

David nodded sheepishly. "Well, consider me there."

"Good!" Dr. Neil turned and began walking back to his golf cart, over his shoulder he said, "Casual, no need to bring anything but yourself and your drinking hat."

David did not know what that meant, but if the rest of the community drank like Dr. Neil, he would not need to be so worried about who saw him. They likely would not remember—or care—either way.

CHAPTER 10

After Dr. Neil clumsily made his way to the golf cart and committed an errant U-turn to return to his own home, David entered his rental from the garage. For the first time, he was able to soak in the entirety of what surrounded him. From where he stood at the barricade which separated the garage and the house put him in the back corner of the kitchen.

The kitchen was brightly lit, but not from any bulbs. Rather, the natural light filling the areas with an impressive hue and warmth reflected in from the hardwood wall in the living room. It was an interesting decorative choice, but it gave the home a true beach house vibe. The kitchen and living room were connected, allowing him to set eyes on the glass wall which ran the entire length of the home, floor to ceiling. Even from his vantage point, he saw nothing but the expansiveness of Lake Michigan, the dark blue water moving rhythmically and without interruption.

Boats could be seen in the distance, but they were too far away to make out what types of boats they were. David then moved his attention to the living room itself. Noting the dark red of the cherry wood flooring which also reflected the light from the sun. A large television hung on the right wall—he guessed seventy inches at least—just above a fireplace. The white leather sofa and loveseat strategically placed in the living room were a nice contrast to the dark floors and fireplace. The kitchen in which he stood had charcoal-colored stone countertops. An island that doubled as a bar blocked him from walking directly into the living room.

The fridge was a steel one, seemingly less expensive than everything else. The oven seemed run-of-the-mill, and the cabinets were spotless, despite their glowing white paint being the most vulnerable of any other surfaces in the house.

David continued his self-guided tour, finding a half bath on the first floor and a simple guest room. It held only a twin bed, a deep black leather recliner in the opposite corner, a television half the size of the one in the living room, and two dressers. One held the television and the other rested on the left side of the bed. The view from this room was a continuation of that in the living room.

He went back into the living room and found the spiral staircase at the far end of the room, initially hidden from his position in the kitchen, blocked by the wall. The stairs were wooden and matched that of the main flooring. Once upstairs he found himself in a maze. The hall broke off in two directions, straight and right. He decided to go straight.

The walls were dressed with pictures of Lake
Michigan, Chicago, and the dunes. Old fashioned
lights hung from the wall, mechanical candles sitting
on a black base spaced every thirty-two inches apart.
Two doors were in this hall, one a guest bedroom
which was set up exactly like the one downstairs.
However, the view was not as majestic, rather, it was
of the tree line to the left of the house. However,
from this vantage point, he was able to tell the woods
were just two rows of trees separating his house from
an empty plot of sand.

The second room was set up as an office. A
Venetian red desk sat pressed to a window
overlooking the lake. The desk had six drawers—
three on either side of the occupant—the bottom on
each side being a double drawer for folders and larger
files. The chair was a pure leather wingback, quite
expensive for a rental home, but it was Havana. The
dark black leather shimmered in the sun and filled the
room with the sweet smell of a fresh car. A lamp
rested on the right side of the otherwise bare desk.
The walls were lined with more snapshots of nearby
nature. There sat a bookcase to the left of the desk
full of books, most of them looked like books left by
past guests or ones the owner of the home had no
more use for, and rather than selling or donating,
used them for decorative props in this office.

The second hall had three rooms. A small
game room with a miniature pool table that converted
into a ping pong table. Another television with a
brown leather loveseat. A bookcase full of board
games and cards. A less than exciting view of sand
and the street, then, Dr. Neil's house, a hundred yards
away.

The next room appeared to be a study. Two
leather wing-back chairs sat opposite each other, but
both cockeyed to the door. A small round wooden
table sat between the two. To the extreme right was
an electric fireplace and a liquor cabinet, stocked and
ready. Liquor and wine glasses were arranged just
right on the top of the case.

On the opposite side of the room was a
bookcase, this one stretching the length of the entire
wall and tall enough to require a rolling ladder. David
did not look closely, but from where he stood, the
books appeared more cared for. Loved. Some of them
bound in leather still uncreased and profound in their
color. Some looked like law books, some like
medical books, and others like novels. He admired
the room longer than the others, if he had a house, he
thought, this was something he would put in it.

Finally, David went into the final room. The
master bedroom. Upon entering he was graced with
another wall-to-wall floor-to-ceiling view of the lake.
A curtain ran the length of the ceiling to conceal the

inhabitant from any passerby down on the beach, though the windows appeared to be tinted. A king-size bed with a pure black frame was placed directly in the center of the window. To his right was a matching black entertainment center with a large—but not as large as downstairs—television. Another dresser sat on the opposite wall and two nightstands stood on either side of the bed.

David made his way to the master bath which stopped him when he entered. The counters were topped with pearl stone, the faucets gold, but untarnished like gold paint would be. A two-person shower rested across from the sinks, with a wall separating the shower from a jacuzzi bath large enough for two or three people to fit. A door across from the tub held a toilet. The door in the center of the back wall held the walk-in closet.

The closet was at least the size of his penthouse living room, he thought. The ceilings were easily ten feet high, and clothing racks lined the entirety of the room. An island surrounded by shoe cubbies sat in the middle of the room and a full-length mirror had been attached to the back wall. Lights were built into the mirror to provide the viewer with the best glimpse of themselves possible.

Once David pulled himself away from the closet he began searching for an entrance to the widow's tower. When he looked at it from the outside, it appeared to have access. A door for someone to walk out and peer out to the lake, even what looked like handrails from a staircase. But David could not find the entry in any of the rooms he had entered already. He thought about going outside to see if he could get a better view but then decided that would have to wait.

He was hungry and needed to eat. And he needed to come up with a story for the party. Something to tell the other guests when they inevitably asked what brought him to their secret little community. And, for the unnerving possibility, he would run into Caroline and Braden.

CHAPTER 11

The next evening David went back and forth for over thirty minutes trying to decide if he should walk to the party or drive. He assumed with the distances separating the houses, people would be driving. Still, it was less than a mile and he did not intend to stay longer than needed. But he doubted the people attending the party would be the type to walk anywhere. Even Dr. Neil rode around in a golf cart.

Finally, David decided to walk. He did not want to risk being blocked in by someone and the hassle that would ensue just for him to leave. His exit would take more time than his walk there and back. David's nerves began to rise in the pit of his gut. He began the breathing technique he had taught hundreds of clients—the same technique that allowed him to make it through his first interview—and felt his muscles relax. His heart rate slowed to a normal range and the fluttering tangle in his stomach slowly subsided.

David had an hour to kill before he would walk down, not wanting to arrive before too many guests. He wanted to be another face in the crowd and the best way to accomplish this was to be later than the bulk of the guests. He went up to the office on the second floor, where he had already set up his laptop, and put down his pad and pen.

Though David was only in his mid-thirties, something about writing notes by hand appealed to him. He never did get used to taking notes on a screen. Even in his practice, he would write his notes by hand and then transcribe them into his processor. He would then return the leather-bound journal to his briefcase until he needed it again. Besides, he liked that if he needed to reference something quickly, he could. No passwords, no scrolling, no keywords. Just flip a page and everything he needed was right there.

At the computer he spent several minutes trying to find a map or pictures of Havana, hoping he could get a lay of the land. To see where all the roads lead. He knew there was a center of town somewhere east, almost like an all-inclusive resort. The people of Havana had all they needed within the gated walls. The only problem, David did not know how to get to any of it. And the state of the blurred map had not changed.

After fifteen minutes he gave up and turned his attention to his journal. He read through his early entries for Caroline and her husband. Things seemed mostly normal and tame for the first three months. They had come in due to poor communication and feeling distant from each other—David knew poor communication was never a real problem.

Understanding what was being communicated was the problem. But then, seemingly out of nowhere, they had returned from a weekend here in Havana—the first they had mentioned their vacation home—and Braden had become fully withdrawn.

He had only attended one session after their return and then it was only Caroline. She had reported he would withdraw more each week. Sometimes even becoming nasty, but never violent. She said he had become a different man as if stress were eating him from the inside out and there was nothing they could do about it. Whatever had happened, whatever caused this change in him, it happened here. And now, he was here.

David arrived at the party nearly a half-hour after it was set to begin. Golf carts lined the driveway and both sides of the street. David was glad he did not drive if for no other reason than he would have felt silly being the only one to drive an actual car. David had found a welcome pamphlet in the rental house that told him there was a cart rental shop in town, he told himself he would rent one the next day. Unfortunately, the pamphlet did not include an address, map, or instructions on how to find the town. It was like an obligatory invitation to dinner but never giving the date or time.

David walked to the front door of the home, a classic beach house-style building. It was different from the one he was staying in, but somehow the same. At the door, he knocked twice, and then took a step back. He could hear the roar of 70s rock and laughter, yelling voices trying to talk over the music and each other. He knocked again, harder this time, and a woman in a bright yellow sundress opened the door.

The woman smiled brightly, her teeth as white and stainless as the cabinets in his kitchen. She was an older woman, and though old age may have begun to steal her hearing, sight, and speed, it had not touched her beauty.

"Why, hello! I do not think we have met; I am Charlette Ogletree." Charlette looked David over once, and then once more. He could tell she was trying to decide if he were a guest or just a tourist who heard the ruckus and had the hope of free booze in his heart.

"I am David Thorne," he said extending his right hand. "I met Dr. Neil yesterday and he told me I should come by."

Charlette leaned her head back with a fake laugh and brought her hand to her chest, foregoing the shake. "My Neil has never met a stranger. I can tell you that much." A look of shock and shame came across her face as she stepped to the side. "And where have my manners gone? Come right on in, Dale?"

"David," he reminded her.

"Right, so drinks are in the kitchen with the food. We had it catered in from Chicago." She looked around at the growing crowd in the room. "Neil is around somewhere. He might be outside with the boys having a cigar. Feel free to make yourself at home."

Before David could thank her—or say anything for that matter—Charlette was swallowed by the crowd. He was left standing alone, but that was a good thing. No one else seemed to notice him at all, which meant he could find what he needed and get out.

David had met two other men and a woman, the only name he remembered was Chanceler Wells, the attorney. He only remembered it because of the tension the man cast into the room. He had casually asked one of the men and the woman about Caroline and her husband, saying, "I did business with them in the past. They mentioned they come here often and it sounded so beautiful. Do you know if they are here?"

The man had not seen them, but the woman thought she had. She told David that when she and her husband were driving into Havana, she thought she saw their car just outside the gates, parked at a grimy-looking establishment that should be ashamed of how terrible it presented itself. She saw Caroline in the passenger seat, but when her husband honked, she did not look up. The woman, however, had not seen them since. That was three days ago.

But Jack had told David that both of their cars were in the garage of their Meridian Hills home. Did they have another car here in Havana?

Chanceler was a burly man. He almost presented as if he were offended that David would ask about them. As if David had broken some sort of unwritten rule. Once the lawyer, drunk but still a lawyer, began to ask questions, David played it off as if he were just a curious wonderer. He broke the conversation by saying he saw an old friend he wanted to catch up with. He doubted the man believed it, but he did not care. As long as he was away from him.

One day in and he had already almost gotten himself caught. David would have made a lousy spy, he mused to himself.

Once David had casually slipped into the background and everyone else had returned to the party, David scanned the house. He had a long hall to his back—the right of the front door—which held three rooms and another hall at the end leading to somewhere unseen. To his right was a spiral staircase that resembled that in his rental. He assumed the upstairs would be the safest place to go. Everyone would be occupied with the party, but if they wandered away, somewhere downstairs is where they would likely find themselves.

David watched the crowd as he made his way up the steps, but he breathed a sigh of relief when he was blocked by a wall of the spiral stairs only a quarter of the way up. The upstairs was somewhat similar to his, an "L" shape with doors along each wall. David hoped to find an office. In an office might be an address book—assuming he was not the only person alive who still kept one—and there he might find what he was looking for.

David made his way to the end of the hall that made the vertical part of the "L" and entered the last room. To his delight, it was Dr. Neil's office, which David knew was the best place to find contact information. People did not keep those in intimate locations, like bedrooms or bathrooms, they kept them where they were most likely to need them.

Dr. Neil's office was as extravagant as every other part of the man's life. Maple wood bookcases lined floor to ceiling with medical texts. Framed accolades and credentials were strategically placed around the room, hanging just right on the cherry walls to draw attention to each one individually, ensuring none would be missed. Dr. Neil's desk was mahogany, a large u-desk with a laptop in the center, a notebook on the right portion, and a printer on the left.

David crept to the desk, ignoring the rest of the office. The desk was pristine, and nothing was allowed out of place. He began opening the drawers, the first two holding miscellaneous papers and documents that did not keep David's attention. The third drawer was in the center of the desk, it slid to where one would keep a keyboard if they had a desktop. Dr. Neil used it to store more notebooks, one of which was an address book, another a calendar. David flipped through the past two weeks of the agenda log but saw nothing about Caroline or Braden. He also did not find their name in the address book.

David began to feel tense. He had been up here far too long. As he turned to leave, something from the bookcase caught his eye. He approached it, holding his breath as if hunting prey, one sound, and the picture would flee in terror. The picture sat in a golden frame right in the center of the closest ledge. He had missed it before, not expecting a picture to be the answer, or figuring it was another of Dr. Neil's accommodations.

The picture showed Dr. Neil arm-in-arm with his wife, Charlette. Beside her, Caroline and Braden also stood arm-in-arm, broad smiles across the quadruplet's faces. The house behind them was the

Baker's, it was the same beach house from the picture in Caroline's Indianapolis home. David squinted to read the address panel between Charlette and Caroline. Nine-two-two.

David repeated the number several times to himself and took a mental picture of the house even though he still had one on his phone.

David let the door to the office open a fraction of an inch, just enough to let one eye peer into the hall. When he was sure he was alone, he left the office, closing the door gently behind him. He made a break for the stairs, not running, but not quite walking either. At the foot of the steps, he nearly collided with a disgusting array of hulas plastered across a broad orange shirt.

"Mr. Thorne?" Dr. Neil was mostly drunk, his confusion was made worse by the fact.

"Oh, Dr. Neil," David said looking around sheepishly.

"What are you doing up here, my good boy?"

David leaned in as if he were about to break a secret of colossal magnitude, but he did not whisper. "I had to take a leak but could not find the bathroom. I was just about to run back home."

"Oh, nonsense," Dr. Neil said with a graveled chuckle. "Last door on the right," he said pointing down the opposite hall David had chosen. "Take your time, I was just going to change my shirt. These class jesters seem to think my shirt is 'tacky'." He emphasized his distaste for their wording with air quotes.

"Thank you, so much. I will see you downstairs. And for the record, I think it makes you look hip."

Dr. Neil smirked and gave David an approving nod as he slid past him toward his room. David went to the bathroom for the show, but it allowed him time to say the address a few more times, this time out loud. "Nine-two-two...Nine-two-two…Nine-two-two."

CHAPTER 12

David spent another thirty minutes at the party before thanking Dr. Neil and his wife for allowing him to enjoy their company. He walked back to his rental, wondering the whole time if someone was following him. Wondering if Dr. Neil questioned his excuse for being upstairs. When he went into his rental home, he left the lights off, allowing the twilight to guide him. From behind a partially closed curtain on the second floor, he watched the road, making sure no one had followed him.

He was not sure where the paranoia formed from. Whether it was doing something he knew was unethical or hearing one too many of Jack's tales, he felt vulnerable. After a few minutes, though, his mind settled and he made his way downstairs to read by the fire.

Even though the night was warm, something about sitting in a recliner with a good book and a dancing flame made David's tensions melt. He was not reading, though. He had spent the last hour wondering if he should find that house from the picture then, or wait. He weighed his options and decided there was no real reason he should not do it now. He would wait for darkness to set over the entire compound and once the music and roaring voices from next door dissipated to inaudible levels, he would make his move.

This happened quicker than he expected—only fifteen minutes after the decision had been made. He repeated the address one more time in his mind, making sure he remembered it—nine-two-two. Then he stepped out onto his back patio. Night suddenly wrapped around him like a thick blanket, covering everything within its grasp, vanishing it into a sea of darkness. He felt small standing there, stars he had not seen in decades became visible, and the crashing of the lake at the shore seemed immense, a Goliath warning David to stay clear.

He figured that he had a better chance of being unnoticed if he walked along the beach than he did walking along the road. The beach remained dark with no noticeable lights present anywhere within his range of sight. The problem, he admitted to himself, was that he did not know where the house was. It may not have even been on this stretch of beach or his road at all.

Even if it were, the house had not been the focus of the picture, so from the front, he would need the address to tell if he had found it. From the back, he knew it would be impossible to tell. He decided to walk along the beach until he saw a house that seemed vacant, he would then wrap around to the front and find the address—hoping no motion lights would be activated.

⁂

The figure almost did not notice the man walking on the beach. He stood in the blood-thorn bushes lost in a chaotic mind running in circles, like a rat trapped in a cage with nothing but one of those wheels to occupy its energy. The figure probably would not have noticed the man, just a hundred yards away, had he not been walking so strangely. He would move quickly for twenty feet or so, then his steps showed trepidation.

The figure did not recognize them—at least not his body type—but then the darkness hid his face well. The man was alone, which made the figure wonder if he was a regular or a vacationer. There was no high-end bitch on his arm, which most men around here would trot along the beach hoping to impress enough to give up some ass. Rarely did the residents just walk the shore at night, definitely not alone.

The figure watched a while more until his task pulled at him. There was a job to finish. The figure knelt in the blood-thorn patch, hiding until the

man left. As the figure did so, one of the rose bushes
stuck into the flesh along the leg, causing the figure
to growl at it. This had become almost second nature,
no one messed with someone that growled in anger.
It scared them. The figure liked that. It gave them
their power without them even realizing it.

David saw the last house on that stretch of the
beach. It looked dark, not white like the house he was
searching for. Wherever that house was, it was not on
this portion of the beach. Then, from the corner of his
eye, something caught his attention. At first, for just a
moment, he thought there was movement in the rose
patch just a hundred yards or less in front of him. He
thought it was an odd place to put a patch of roses, at
least such a large patch.

But what caught his eye was beyond that,
partially obscured by the tree line behind the rose
patch. He noticed a large boat very close to shore.
Then he noticed there was a dock there. It looked as
out of place as a black ink spot on a white shirt. The
entire expanse of the beach in each direction was
nothing but sand and water. Then in that one section
was a dock, more like a miniature pier, he thought.
David could not see what was happening at the dock

or with the boat, perhaps delivering goods for the local mart. But it seemed far too late for that.

David decided to return to his retreat and sleep. He would look for the house with the guidance of light.

CHAPTER 13

David rolled over to the sun greeting him. He stretched in the plush bed which sucked consciousness out of him as soon as he laid on it the night before. Remnants of a dream tugged at the edge of his memory, he thought it was a good dream, but he could not be sure. Flashes of faces and some old buildings ran through his mind, but they meant nothing. Then, it was gone. Forgotten like an old phone number unused and unneeded.

The sun shining through the window was warm, and pleasant on his body as he groaned. He grabbed his phone to check the time, he rarely slept without an alarm, and even then, it was an anomaly for him to sleep in. He was somewhat surprised to see it was 10 a.m., but he did not mind. His body and brain needed the rest and he was supposed to be on vacation after all.

David got out of bed and stared out at the lake for a few moments. The water was as blue as it was calm, almost looking like a mirror on the edge of the land. It was a wonder to him, after all these years, he could still be amazed by this state. The outside world thought of Indiana as cornfields and little else. But David knew that the terrain in Indiana was vast and different much like the entire country. Here in the north, you had Lake Michigan which could make you think you were in Florida. In the south, you had thick woods and rolling hills, waterfalls, and deep caves. In the middle you had a big city, small towns, and yes, corn fields. But also, so much more.

David broke his concentration, ready for the day. He dressed quickly in a pair of khaki shorts, a plain white tee shirt, and some loafers. He did not quite look like a beach bum, but he also did not feel like he would stand out.

After his coffee and a quick bite of his bagel, both of which he prepared while he washed his face and corrected the mess the bed had made of his hair, he went into the backyard. Tucked close to the house was a shed. He would have never known it was there, except he spotted it from the beach when he had returned from his failed search the night before.

Inside the shed, there were some beach chairs, some inflatables, a volleyball set, and a beach cruiser bicycle. He figured he would be less noticeable on a bike than in his car, and the compound likely was not large enough to require a car anyhow. The bike looked new, or at the very least, hardly used. The tires were full and still had the vent spews. The bike had a metal basket screwed to the handlebars and the wide seat looked like it would make for a comfortable ride.

Five minutes later he was at the front of the house ready to take off. He looked down the road trying to visualize the layout of the compound. He knew that the road he was on had a left-hand turn about two miles down, which he hoped would lead to more houses and the center of town. He had seen the boat docking in that direction the night before and he knew that town was on the right side if looking from the outside of the front gate. The directions he had been given to reach the house did not mention how to get to town, or where any of the nameless roads led, making the journey more of a challenge.

Ten minutes later David had gone the two miles where the road split. The left turn took a drastic uphill approach which David dreaded before even making the turn. It looked near vertical and at least thirty yards up. The road was narrow making the treacherous climb even more deceitful as he would not know if a car was coming or if the road continued up from where it vanished. Unlike a road bike, this one did not have any gears to assist his ascent. He stood on the pegs and began peddling hard.

At the top he collapsed in the seat, his chest pounding like a snare, sweat pouring by the liter from his scalp. His white shirt became soaked everywhere it touched his skin and his lungs burned for oxygen, begging for more but finding none. Once he reached the crest of the hill, sure that no cars would wipe him off the road, he peddled to the edge.

He sat there for several minutes catching his breath, and allowing his mind to slow down enough to inspect his surroundings. It was as if he had been transported to another world, the beachscape had given way to a small forest. Tall trees surrounded the road on either side. In front of him was a steep slope just as impressive as the ascent, but beyond were four more houses, and then a town.

CHAPTER 14

David passed the houses to his left and found the house he was looking for to be the second one he passed. He did not get to look at it long, but he did not see any cars in the driveway and it did not look like anyone had been walking on the sandy property within the past few days. Maybe longer. He did not want to stop to get a closer look in the middle of the morning, knowing someone would see him and it would raise suspicion—an outsider snooping around a resident's house.

Instead, he barreled down the hill only hoping he would be able to control the bicycle, now possessed by the powers of gravity and brakes designed for minimalistic speeds. The town was less than a hundred yards from him, closing in more and more. Though he did not consciously notice it, a brief realization he hardly caught came to his mind. There were no cars in town.

There were bikes or golf carts. It was a strange sight, but he did not have time to think much more about it before returning his focus to the road which came to a switch-back before returning true into town. He came to the switch-back which went left then right at near ninety-degree angles before leveling off to a flat road, just twenty yards from town.

David leaned the bike low to the left sure that the tires would find sand and slip from under him, sending him cascading to the ground like an errant ball. Just before his peddles scraped pavement he flipped the bike over to the right gripping the handlebars so tightly the rubber of the grips mushed beneath his palms. As he began to straighten the bike, the rear tire ultimately found the sand it had avoided on the previous turn. His tire slid left, then right, and then self-corrected.

As the road flattened his speed declined gradually, still ignoring the brakes no matter how hard he tried to use them. After a few yards, his speed was no longer life-threatening or neck-breaking. He was then able to soak in some of the sights around him, trying to get a lay of the land. To his left, he would soon pass a large wooden building. POSTAL SERVICE + SHIPPING was painted in bold red paint across the face of the wooden building, which he could now tell looked like a barn. It was tall and wide with no windows that he could see and a large garage door in the center, a typical white door to the left of that.

Behind the building, he saw a long boardwalk that led from the back of the building, down the beach, to a large dock at the edge of the water This was likely where he had seen the boat docking the night before. Either supplies for the community or residents' mail coming or going. Either way, he decided to view the rest of town.

The road he was on led straight to a fountain standing fifteen feet tall. It was a statue of a man and water poured from a jar on his shoulder into the water resting in a round basin beneath him. The road split right and left around the fountain, not quite a roundabout, rather a split in the street. David rode past the fountain and found a bicycle parking spot just beyond it. The rack sat in an open grass area that looked like a park, nestled between two rows of businesses.

The side of the road he was on held a police station, clothing store, printing facility, and the courthouse. Across the street were a diner, a small theater, a bakery, and a grocery store that in any other place would have looked insufficient and minute. However, in Havana, it seemed perfect. The whole layout reminded David of a small east coast town more than it reminded him of a beach town, like much of how the rest of the compound tried to come across. He stopped the bike to admire the sight.

David was so occupied taking in the setting that he did not notice the police officer approaching him from across the street. Not until the man spoke, "Morning." His voice was chipper and relaxed. He was a man with an easy job—fighting crime in a crimeless town.

"Morning," David returned.

The man stuck a hand out for David to shake. He looked like the kind of person that judged a man based on their shake. David caught sight of the gun on the cop's waist, which, unlike the size of the grocery store, did seem out of place. The piece looked like a prop to finalize the authenticity of a Halloween costume more than an actual tool the officer would ever use.

"I'm Deputy Carl Ringwall. You can just call me, Carl." Deputy Carl looked David over once, and then again. "Don't think I've seen you around here."

"I rented one of the properties at the other end. Staying a few days."

Carl smiled and nodded, not looking particularly interested in what David had to say. Carl looked almost too young to be a sworn officer. His hair was dark and combed back like a 50's gangster, but his face only showed patches of peach fuzz. He was an athletic man, however, and David was sure that if he wanted, he could make David pay for any snide remarks. "Most of the renters stay in their houses during their stay."

"Really? Never come to the store or the diner?"

Carl's smirk widened, "Nope, usually grab whatever they'll need on the way in."

Seems ridiculous, David thought, "Well, I have never been much of a homebody. A day as beautiful as today I thought it would be nice to get out and explore a little."

"I bet…" The smirk had faded now and the deputy's eyes narrowed, but before he could unleash on David, another officer appeared from nowhere. At least, David had not seen him.

"Hello there!" This officer was older than the deputy, a little older than David himself, but not by much. His hair had already begun to grey at the sides and his time as an officer in Havana obviously left him doing most of his work from a desk. His frame showed remnants of a man who once may have looked quite intimidating but now looked to have softened. His jawline was still pronounced and his dark green eyes seemed to push cheerfulness. But his weight mostly rested in his stomach.

"Hello, officer," David said.

"Sheriff Tom," Carl said. "I was just talking to the newest visitor of our little town here."

"It is a beauty, isn't it?" Tom took in a deep breath of the summer morning's air before releasing it with a trace of fresh coffee.

"I don't think that word even attempts to do it justice."

Tom's smile widened, "Well, if you need anything while you're here, you just let me know. If I may make a suggestion," Tom said and put his hands out as if giving a gift to David.

"Please."

"If you go to the diner order the Ruben. And be sure to check out the theater if you are here this weekend. They are showing Jaws and it is free popcorn night."

"I wouldn't miss that for the world." David felt a sense of relief talking to Tom over Carl. The deputy gave off a tense vibe, but it was not the kind he felt when clients in court-ordered therapy would make empty threats to try and intimidate David to sign their documents. Of course, he had not had to worry about that since opening his practice. The deputy felt different, though. He felt like a man of his word.

"How long did you say you were staying?" Deputy Carl asked.

"A few days."

"Leave the man alone, Carl. He's a guest." Sheriff Tom handed David a card. David looked it over and found his name and a number, the emblem of the Havana Sheriff's Department plastered smack in the center of the cream-colored card.

"So, Havana has their own police force, huh? Get much crime?"

Carl's eyes narrowed and the man looked as if he were about to growl and pounce on the prey. Tom, on the other hand, chuckled. "Not even remotely. But as you might imagine it makes the folks around here feel better just knowing there is a police presence. After all, they leave their private security on the other side of the gate."

David wanted to ask why they even let outsiders in if that were the case. But he let it go. Instead, he thanked Tom for his hospitality and promised to try the Ruben. The two officers headed in the opposite direction to the police station just yards away.

§

He looked across his desk at the figure. It was intimidating, nothing short of fear-provoking to anyone who crossed its path. But to him, the form was harmless, the form answered to him, and if that was the arrangement, he did not need to fear it. A nameless being recognized by many but known by none, one that did as it was told and did it well.

"Did you handle our little problem?"

"Yeah," the form's voice was low and steady never betraying a hint of emotion. Never mad, never happy, it just was. "He won't be fucking things up anymore."

"And his wife?"

"I have special plans for her."

He slammed his hand on the table, but the figure across from his desk did not flinch. The empty eyes did not even blink. "Dammit! I told you to take care of her! We cannot have any loose ends!"

"It's tight as a knot. She isn't going nowhere."

"Listen to me," he put his index finger and thumb a fraction of an inch from each other to illustrate his point. "We are this close to the biggest payday of our lives. If she fucks this up, it's your ass!"

The figure across from him smiled a tempting smile. As if to say, "I dare you." Then the smile widened slightly as the form stood and leaned across the desk, the weight of its body being held up by hands planted firmly on the top of the desk. The desk pleaded under the weight. The grin now double-dared him to keep this promise.

"Look," he said, taking half a step back. "I just want to make sure that this happens and then we can all make a lot of money. Then you and I are done. Clear?"

"As crystal."

The figure turned its back to him and left the office. When it was gone, a denseness that had occupied the office just moments before, dissipated.

The room seemed brighter and the air a bit fresher. He sat down in his leather chair and opened the drawer at the face of his desk, revealing a snub-nosed revolver. A .38 his father had given him when he was sixteen.

When he saw it, he felt comforted. Then he thought about his father. The burley car salesman who made a fortune flipping cars and then real estate. The fortune allowed them to purchase the plot of land that eventually became Havana. His father could be a loving and doting father on Monday, and by Tuesday be the biggest bastard in the world. One whiskey too many and his hand would eventually find the flesh on the man's face. Unless his mother stepped in, which she did sometimes. Then she would take the punishment. But it was because of his father that he was the man he had become. Strong, wealthy, business savvy, and prepared for the darkness of the world. And a servant in his own way.

Every time he saw the gun the reaction was the same. Thinking about a man he both adored and hated. A man he missed and despised. A man whose tragic death he still mourned, but which he had also caused. With that very same revolver.

CHAPTER 15

David had spent several hours scanning through his notes from the sessions he and Caroline had over the previous six months. He scanned them time and time again, each stretch hoping he would find something he had overlooked before. Something she had said, something in her body language, even something from Braden when he had been in session. But each time was just as fruitless as the one before it.

He was not entirely sure what he was hoping to find. He would not have been able to narrow it down to an exact designation if he had a gun to his head. Throughout their time together, Braden seemed to grow more distant from Caroline. The flame that roared between them dwindled to a soft glow, and then during their last session, Caroline had suggested the flame extinguished.

It was not surprising they had relationship issues. They had sought him out after all. But their situation was atypical. Sure, couples would come to therapy and some would never resolve their issues, deciding it would be better to cut their losses than to keep fighting a losing battle. But he had never seen a couple—who by all accounts was not *that* volatile—

self-implode as the Baker's had. Sure, they had been struggling, he thought, but the decision to end the marriage seemed to be the dramatic end to that slow burn. But maybe that was not the end of it. Maybe something else had happened when she brought up her desire to leave.

Caroline had never mentioned an affair, in fact, from his notes, it seemed like the thought had never crossed her mind. His behavior resembled that of a man caught in a torrent affair—sneaking off in the middle of the night, distancing himself emotionally and physically, becoming mentally vacant—and still, she only felt they had grown apart. Caroline knew Braden better than he did, and David would not accuse the man of something his wife had shown no concern about.

Then something tugged at the rim of David's unconscious. Something Caroline had said, almost as an afterthought, and to which David made no note. He closed his eyes and put the butt of his hands to his temples, applying steady pressure to his skull. Something he often did to recall a memory just outside of his recollection. Then it came to him.

"We have always been pretty well off," Caroline had said. "But once we got the lake house, Braden struck gold, another sign it was supposed to help. He made more two months after we bought the property than he had the entire second half of last year."

"Finances can certainly be a struggle for many couples. More so when you buy a new house and are also trying to get pregnant. It is good that does not seem to be an issue here."

Caroline shrugged. "Yeah, but he seems to work more when we are at the lake house than when he is here. Always has meetings in town."

Rather than exploring that further, David focused on how lonely she must have felt in those situations. How hard it must have been to have everything she thought she had wanted, yet nothing she desired.

That conversation meant something. He could feel it. What had Braden's new business venture been? Why did it start here in Havana?

David finally opened his eyes and realized the sun was setting. A golden hue had been cast over the lake from the west, hints of red and blue artfully splashed about the landscape. He closed his notebook and latched the lock, then stood from his seat, down the hall, down the steps two at a time, and out of the front door. He hoped he would have enough light to navigate the treacherous hill and arrive under the cover of night.

David pulled the bike into the Baker's driveway, loose gravel crunched under the weight of the tires and David instinctively looked back to the police station. Even at its distance, it felt as though it towered above him. At the end of the drive, he leaped from his seat and lifted the bike into his arms. Thankful for the light weight of the aluminum frame, he carried it with him around to the back of the house.

Square pavers had been placed in the sand two feet apart from one another. It provided a well-directed path to the rear of the house and prevented him from leaving any tracks. At the rear of the house, David placed the bike on the wooden deck which still smelled of sealant and stain. He lifted each foot until he was satisfied that the deck, though fresh, was not sticking to his shoes.

David scanned around ensuring he was covered. To his right, he could see the end of the dock where shipments would arrive. The view was less obstructed than it had been the night before from the other side of the tree line. To his left was the town, lights shimmered through but did not penetrate the brush line enough to betray his activities.

David tried the door but found it locked. He was not surprised—though part of him was. Havana did not seem like the type of place people made a habit of locking doors. He looked down at his feet disappointed. No mat meant no key. He stuck his face to the glass of the door and though the night was growing darker by the second and the house was void of light, he could make out that no food or cookware was out. No dishes were in the sink. It looked as though no one had been there in some time.

David turned, ready to leave, defeated and rethinking his reason for coming to Havana. Then he spotted a rock. It was a little rock sitting in the sand just off the deck. It looked out of place and unnatural on the otherwise barren beachfront. He did not see another rock anywhere near the house. He stepped down to the closest paver and squatted as low as he could, using his left hand as a kickstand to maintain his balance.

He leaned desperately for the stone, not wanting to touch the sand resting between him and the rock. His finger swiped the top of it and instantaneously he felt the familiar texture of plastic. He stretched again, groaning as his latissimus muscle screamed. Finally, he was able to get just enough pressure on the rock to roll it a few inches closer. Then closer. And then he was able to grab it.

The bottom had a latched compartment which he opened with ease and found a key. It was an odd way to try and hide a key, but David assumed it was more a factor of convenience than security.

Within seconds David was in the house. From where he stood it did not seem like any of the windows had blinds, at least not in the kitchen. He could not blame them, though, the view was not one to be hidden. However, it meant he would not be able to turn on any lights or use his flashlight. He would be wandering in the dark.

The home had an open floor plan, for which he was grateful. And unlike his rental and Dr. Neil's house, it was ranch-style, which meant he would not have to stumble through the dark for as long. He stood in the kitchen a moment, allowing his eyes to adjust to the blackness. From what he could tell, the kitchen opened to a living room—or maybe a sitting room—and to the right was a wide hallway that broke into two directions. One, he assumed, would wrap around to the living room. The other veered right, which would be where he would find something if he were to find anything at all.

David crept across the hardwood flooring, careful to make as little noise as possible. Even though by all appearances the house was empty, the last thing he needed would be for his clients to catch him sneaking into their house.

When David reached the hall, he peered out into the living room. It was dark and vacant, the television a large mass against the wall. A coffee table rested a foot from a dark sofa and in the corner across from him was a recliner. The front door rested just left of that.

David began his cautious walk again, down the hall which had four doors—all closed—two on either side. He went to the first door on his left, twisting the knob gently, pausing each time the latch clicked. David eased the door open inch, by agonizing inch. His breath hung in his chest and his head began to throb from the lack of oxygen.

Once the door was open enough for him to look inside, he found a bathroom. It was made-up and orderly, not even a used towel hanging from the shower. He slid the upper half of his body into the bathroom and looked at the tub. In the darkness, it was hard to tell, but he thought it looked bone dry.

He slid his body back into the hall and gently closed the door as it had been. He turned and went to the room on the right. The room was also vacant. A quaint guest room with a twin-sized bed and some miscellaneous furniture. The next room to the left was the master bedroom. As soon as David saw the king-sized bed he ducked back into the hall. His brow now sweating profusely, his heart threatening to burst through his sternum.

He took two deep breaths and put his head back in through the crack. The covers on the bed were flat. The room was vacant. He slowly closed the door and turned to the last door in the hall. It was also empty, an office with an L-shaped desk at the window, a large monitor in the center, and cabinet drawers lining the two walls to his right. The left wall had framed items he could not make out.

David slid into the office and went to one of the framed items. It was a degree in law from Stanford University. Braden's degree. David had a gut feeling that whatever had caused Braden to begin withdrawing from Caroline would be in this office. Unless he had already disposed of it. But even if he had, there may be something in the office that would give insight into why they disappeared. Something they were running from, something someone could not let get out, something worth vanishing over.

David began directly to his right and went to each drawer. Opening them and fumbling through the contents, uncertain of what to look for in the first place. Many of the drawers were empty, some had books without anything hidden in them, and others had envelopes that looked like bills or alumni material. He found business forms but nothing which seemed immoral.

Once he reached the desk, he was disappointed to find more of the same. He sat in the chair, finally able to breathe, feeling as though any threat of being caught were no longer pertinent. He sighed heavily in disappointment. The final dead-end that would send him back with no more answers and even more guilt at his idiocy.

David kicked his foot to the side of the desk as he spun around to stand. There was a thud and then another thud as something fell to the floor. David's flesh grew cold and the coldness seeped through his skin into his blood. He looked down to the source of the noise and on the ground was a rectangular piece of wood about ten inches by seven inches. David kneeled from the chair and pulled his phone from his pocket, fumbling to turn on the flashlight.

He did not care if someone saw his light—as improbable as it was from his position—he wanted to know what Braden was hiding in the desk. Inside the void was a leatherbound notebook. What would he need to hide in a secret compartment of his desk? What information would Braden want to keep hidden in such an arbitrary place?

He opened the notebook to the first page when he heard the latch from the backdoor click.

CHAPTER 16

David's chest thudded behind his ribs again, this time with such force that his chest ached. Sweat began to pool on his scalp when he heard heavy footsteps thundering in the kitchen. He grabbed the piece of wood from the floor and slid it back into place, hoping that he had done so correctly. He flipped his flashlight off leaving him in pitch blackness, his eyes could not adjust quickly. He could only see inches in front of his face.

The footsteps stopped and he began skimming the room. He looked back under the desk and noticed that the L portion of the desk appeared to have a hollow spot that might conceal him. There was nowhere for him to go and nothing else that may conceal him if whoever was in the house came into the office. He dropped to his knees and crawled under the desk and back into the cavern of the desk. The space was cramped and part of him began cursing himself for not just jumping out of the window and making a run for it. Even if someone knew he had, they would not know it was *him*. Of course, he was an outsider in Havana, if Braden or Caroline reported a break-in, the cheerful Deputy

Ringwall would be all-too-happy to introduce David's skull to his baton.

Before he could imagine it, the office door swung open. He saw glints of light sweep under the desk and he pulled his legs in closer. Whoever it was, they did not live here. The intruder moved with thunderous steps. They opened, shuffled, and slammed drawers in rapid succession. They, unlike David, knew that no one would be walking in on them.

The weighty steps grew closer to David's hiding space. He thought he could hear his thudding heart echo in his little cave. The drawers on the desk were being opened now and David clinched his jaws, biting the tip of his tongue to ensure silence. The intruder would slam the drawers shut, each time sending a ringing through David's ears.

When the noise stopped David could hear the intruder breathing heavily. The breaths were not as if the trespasser were out of shape, but as if they were angry. Enraged by the fact that whatever they came for was not there. Then David felt the leather in his hands and clinched the book tight to his chest.

The light suddenly exploded under the desk and David bit down hard on his cheek. He could taste the copper tang of blood on his tongue. The light danced left to right and then disappeared.

"Fuck!" The voice was deep and angry. The word came out more as an animalistic growl than a form of human language.

David then heard the footfalls distance themselves from him and then the door to the office swung open, slamming into the wall. Then the intruder slammed the door hard as they left.

David let out the breath he had been holding in his lungs, trying to keep his gasps quiet. He pressed his right thumb against the lesions in his cheek, stopping any more blood from violating his tastebuds.

David could hear more doors opening, ruffling, rummaging, cursing, and then doors slamming. Several minutes—or in David's mind hours—passed before he heard the enduring steps make their way back through the kitchen where more rummaging ensued. Then he heard the back door open and close. David's left leg and butt cheek tingled and a sharp pain shot down from his buttocks to his left foot when he stretched them. He shook them gently, not wanting to make too much noise in case the invader had not left.

He sat there for another fifteen minutes before circulation had been fully restored and he felt comfortable trying to leave.

"Shit," he mumbled to himself. "No way they didn't see the bicycle." David hoped that whoever had been in the house would assume it belonged to the Baker's. But if they returned and the bike was not there, then what? Or, if they saw him riding it around town. David shook the thought from his mind, there was nothing he could do about that right now.

He would ride back to the house as quickly as he could and store the bike in the garage.

Once David was outside, he tucked the notebook into his back pocket and lifted the bike back into his arms to carry it around the house. But he stopped when he noticed commotion off to his left.

A substantial boat was docked at the delivery port. Lights from the boat shone onto the dock revealing five men carrying large packages, they were speaking loudly but the distance between them and David made the task of understanding them impossible. David could not tell what the group was unloading, but he could just make out the wording on the side of the ship. *Fresh. All natural.* Whatever was written under it was obscured by the dock and the rapid movement of the dockhands.

David broke his gaze from the delivery and stepped out onto the first paver, praying that whoever also broke in, was long gone.

CHAPTER 17

When David woke the next morning at eight, his whole body felt heavy. His eyes screamed at him and there was an intense burn in them as if each blink ground sand into his retinas. He could sense the beginnings of a headache as well. When he looked at his phone, he groaned at the realization he had only slept for two hours.

When he returned to the rental the night before it had been a little past eleven. He wheeled the bicycle into the garage and tried to hide it behind some beach chairs, paranoid that the intruder might happen to see it if they passed the property. He went through the house locking every window and each door. Then, he went back through the house twice more to check his work.

He had not seen anyone else on the road when he left the Baker's and the few houses he passed were as dark as the night around him. Still, whoever had been in there could have been watching. Waiting.

Once he was sure the house was secure, he went up to the bedroom—locking the door behind him—and sat on the plush bed. He opened the leatherbound notebook and began going page by page. It had been used as some sort of ledger. Long lines separated the pages into three categories. To the extreme left were rows of initials, in the center what David thought were dates, and to the right were dollar amounts.

Even one mystery novel would tell him the ledger was tracking illegal activity. Guns, drugs, sex slaves, any number of foul dealings that could have made Braden very rich very quickly. Also, dealings that if gone bad, could cause him to disappear. Voluntarily or otherwise. The notebook dated back four months but was nearly full, each page front and back. There were likely close to sixty pages, David guessed at least two-thousand entries.

None of it made sense to him though. The prices were all over the place. Twenty dollars. Two-hundred. Five-Thousand. One was for twenty-thousand. One thing David did figure out, however, was that all the initials were the same. There were six different initials spread across all two-thousand entries.

David had tried calling Jack—twice—to get his take, but he did not answer. Of course, he had real cases to work on. For all David knew, and he recognized Jack would bring up, these entries were for one of his two legitimate businesses. But if so, why hide it? Why would someone break in to find it?

Maybe they weren't looking for that. Jack would say.

The voice of reason came from a man who had worked hundreds of murder and drug cases. A man who required nothing less than concrete evidence to convince him of anything not blatantly obvious.

David felt his stomach begin to ache. He was hungry but did not feel like cooking. He decided he would head into town and visit the diner—unfortunately walking—and from there plan his next move.

By the time David got into town the temperature already appeared to be flirting with ninety. The town also seemed smaller than it had the day before. Not that the town came across as large, but it felt more closed in than it had just hours previously.

David went into the diner, half expecting an establishment trapped in the 50s. Untouched by time and not perverted by the changes through the decades. Then he half expected to find a low-end Ritz-style diner with a bar trimmed in gold and topped with marble. Instead, he found neither. The diner had four rows of seating each one with three tables. The tables were more than capable of sitting 4 adults. The front counter had a cashier station and a carry-out window with paper menus stacked a foot high.

The floor was tile, not fancy or glamorous, but not offensive and outdated either. Pictures of the lake, boats, fishermen, beach houses, and smiling families he did not recognize were scattered around the walls. In place of the hostess stand was a sign, *Please Seat Yourself.* He did, at the table furthest from him which had a view of the lake from a small window on the back wall. From his seat, he spotted a hallway that led to the bathrooms and the kitchen.

From the hall, with precise timing a woman only a year or two younger than David emerged from swinging doors he could not see from his seat. She wore her dark blond hair up in a tight bun, and a narrow patch of curled hair hung over her right eye. Her uniform was a blue and white striped dress which flattered her figure but did not boast it. A white apron hung from her neck which made her skin appear much more tanned than it probably was. As she grew closer, he noticed her eyes were a sparkling green, letting off a shimmer like a pristine lake in a mountainside clearing.

"Good morning," she said. Her voice was gentle and warm. David was transfixed on her, hardly recognizing that she had even spoken to him. "Are you okay?" She asked, a hint of concern in her voice.

David shook his head. "I am fine. Sorry, not much sleep was had last night."

She smiled and let out a gentle chuckle. She brushed the stray band of hair behind her right ear and then handed David a menu. "We are serving breakfast," she said, "But lunch will be open in ten minutes. If you see something you like, I can get the cooks to start it a little early."

"Breakfast sounds perfect, actually, miss…"

"Bella," she said, smiling again.

"Beautiful." David felt nervous about how the word sounded when it left his mouth. "Bella is Latin for beautiful, isn't it? I am David."

Bella beamed, "It is. I haven't seen you around here before. Did you just buy a house in Havana?"

"Oh no," David said, feeling his face turn warm. "I am renting a house."

"Oh," Bella's eyes widened and her smile curved in as if she were impressed. "Renters don't come into town very often. Of course, not many renters come to Havana to begin with."

"Is that so? How come? It is a beautiful place."

"Couldn't say," she told him, "I have heard most people cannot afford it. I have also heard the vetting process is no cakewalk." She leaned back on her left leg and crossed her arms as if inspecting his reaction to her words.

"I can attest to that," he told her with a grin. "So, what do you recommend, Bella?"

"The waffles with bacon are to die for."

"I'm in a living kind of mood today."

"Then I would recommend the Nature Platter. Organic eggs, plain oatmeal, and fruit."

David laughed, "Waffles it is. Can I also get a black coffee?"

"I'll bring you two, looks like you could use it."

Bella vanished back into the hall with the menu and he wished she had not. David's wish was granted just a second later when Bella returned with a tall cup of steaming coffee and a pink pitcher, which she promised she had just topped off with a fresh pot. Another minute passed and she returned with his breakfast.

He had not appreciated how hungry he had been until he wolfed down the plate of buttered waffles and bacon. Not his typical fair, much sweeter than he normally ate. But it was delicious and dare he think, to die for.

Bella returned with a stained sheet of yellow paper with his due written on the bottom. "I can ring you out when you are ready. No rush though." The way she smiled at the end of her sentence made David enter analysis mode. Something he hated doing, but something which had become second nature to him through the years.

"I must get going, unfortunately. That was wonderful, though. Thank you for the recommendation."

David followed Bella to the front of the diner, she disappeared into the hall as David continued to the cashier counter. Seconds later Bella stood before him typing into the iPad. "Five dollars," she told him.

"That's it?"

"Afraid so."

David handed her a twenty. "Keep the change."

Bella smiled, "How sweet."

As David turned to leave, Bella spoke again. "Listen," she said, her voice more unsure, which had been different from the joking tone she had since he had arrived. "I don't ever do this, but if you would like a tour of Havana, I get off at eight."

David smiled and again felt heat rise in his cheeks. "I will see you then, Bella."

David headed for the door again when Deputy Ringwall and a man resembling a grizzly bear before hibernation entered.

"Well, if it isn't our esteemed guest, Mr. Torn," Ringwall smirked.

David smiled politely, making sure to not make eye contact with the bear for fear it may strike. "It's Thorne. A pleasure to see you again, Deputy."

Before Ringwall could say anything else, David excused himself and squeezed between the bigfoot impersonator and the deputy, escaping into the summer heat. He heard a burly voice he assumed belonged to the bear, "Hey, Bella, bring your pretty self over here, doll. And some coffee too."

CHAPTER 18

David spent some time down at the beach. He utilized it to work on notes for his next lecture. After which, he even spent time cleaning the already spotless kitchen. Anything he could find to get his mind off the ledger, he tried. He always thought more clearly when he gave his mind time to be blank and to focus on the mundane. He knew if he spent more time staring at the pages trying to decipher the meaning behind each letter and number, he would get further from the answer.

At a quarter past two, he heard a knock on his door. His palms instantly began to sweat. There was no reason for anyone—at least no reason which he could fathom—for someone to be knocking on his door. Quickly, and nervously, he ran through his mind a mental checklist. Had he remembered to close the garage door? Had he left something at the Baker's house? Had someone seen him leaving?

He steeled his back and went to the door. The colored glass on the door was not much for allowing visual identification through the door, but he could tell whoever was on the other side was not much bigger than himself. It certainly was not the monstrous man thundering around the house the night before. Before he opened the door completely, he was already giving an invite, "Dr, Neil, come on in."

"Wow, how did you know it was me?"

"You are one of the few people I can think of in Havana that might stop by." David slid to the side allowing room for Dr. Neil to enter. The retired doctor sported the same beach bum outfit as the day before. David wondered if it were the same, or if the man just had a closet full of tacky Hawaiian shirts and khaki shorts.

"One of the few? Made some friends, have you?"

"You," David said, "and Bella, at the diner."

Dr. Neil's eyes widened; a mischievous grin followed. "Oh, pray tell, old boy! I know some geezers around here that have been trying to flirt with her for some time."

"Nothing to tell." David headed for the kitchen and Dr. Neil followed closely. His ears perked like a schoolboy listening steadfastly for the sounds of Santa sneaking down the chimney. David reached the counter, revealing a bottle of cognac that rested in a neat cabinet with glasses. He poured two.

"I was having breakfast at the diner, she was friendly. She offered to give me a tour of Havana after her shift."

Dr. Neil clapped eagerly and then grabbed the closest glass to him, taking a hardy drink. "Won't be much of a tour, my boy. Havana is not very large. There are some neat places for the nature lovers, but for us city folk, what you see is what you get."

"How so?"

"Well, you have downtown, you have the houses scattered about. Then there's a casino and golf course at the far end down that way," Dr. Neil pointed to the right, in the direction of town. "We have a hiking trail out that way as well and a blood-thorn patch."

"Blood-thorn patch? What is that?"

"Rosa Omeiensis. The blood-thorn rose. Just down the beach, there is a patch of it, they brought in special soil to put over the sand and everything. They have beautiful white flowers that come out through June and July, so you can still see them if you head down there. But the stems are a deep blood-red color. Hence the name blood-thorn roses."

"Interesting, I have never heard of those. Why did they put them there to grow? Seems like an odd place, on a beach."

Dr. Neil shrugged. "They wanted it to be kind of a 'state flower' for Havana. Something unique. Most of this area inside the gates is sand, so I guess they thought the beach would be as good a place as any. Plus," he said taking a sip, "on the beach any outsider passing by can see them and be left with even more questions about old Havana."

"Hey," David said returning his thoughts now to Bella. "I didn't see any place in town to rent golf carts. Can you point me in that direction?"

"My place."

"I couldn't, Dr. Neil."

"Nonsense, boy! If you are taking miss Bella around town you need the best damn cart this place has to offer." A smug smile turned up on his face, "Just so happens, I own it."

Jack slammed his phone down on his desk. His tenth call had been ignored and since eight that morning, he had not had time to return David's calls.

"What's wrong, Detective?" The voice came from behind Jack. It was direct but weathered. Jack knew who it was before he even turned around. Retired Detective Daniel Willows stood with his left knee bent, a cane to his left supporting the weight of his body as he leaned on it for stability.

Daniel had retired four years before and instantly became a volunteer officer. Though he mostly just hung around chatting with other cops and groaning about the golden era of policing. The bullet in his left hip forced him to retire. He would have been happy to die at his desk pushing papers. Daniel loved policing as much as he hated his wife, and while most people fanaticized about retirement and spending more time with their families, he dreaded it and promised he would be dead within weeks if he had to stay home.

"Cheddar is dodging my calls," Jack told him.

"Your informant?"

"Yeah."

"You're not in narcotics anymore, what do you care?"

"That murder over on Mass Ave, it looks drug-related. If anyone knows something about something, it's Cheddar." When Jack had worked his first three years as a detective, he worked narcotics. He had busted Cheddar for selling crack and the skinny dope dealer folded at the first opportunity that presented itself. Since then, Jack still called on Cheddar for information whenever he thought drugs were at the root of a case. Until that day, Cheddar always came through. He had helped put away at least half as many thugs and murderers as Jack himself.

"That was a nasty scene according to some of the boys. If Cheddar does know something, he probably knows what those fuckers are capable of. This might be one horse he doesn't want to be on the dick end of. If you were a low-end crack dealer wanting to stay in the dark, where would you hide?"

Daniel had a way of giving other officers the answers they were looking for without giving it to them in black and white. He wanted the officer to feel like they had come up with the answer on their own, and because of this, everyone respected Daniel's input. They never questioned him or brushed him off. Even the young detectives who could be his grandchildren would listen to him and soak up anything he offered.

"There're a couple of spots he likes to hang low at. The catacombs under Market and the Ritz Theater."

"Need a tag-along? Been a hell of a time since I saw any action and to be frank, that seat is killing my ass."

"Sorry, old man, not this time. I do not need to be carrying you on my shoulder when you throw out your other hip."

"Hey now, better watch how you talk to a crotchety old man with a cane. A good way to get yourself hurt, Detective."

Jack smirked at the empty threat, "I will call you if I find anything. Can you let Cap know where I will be if he asks? I have had my quota for ass-chewing this month."

"Sure," Daniel guaranteed. "Oh, and don't get yourself shot. It's a real son-of-a-bitch."

"I'll see what I can do."

CHAPTER 19

David arrived at the diner ten minutes before eight. Dr. Neil had spent an hour teaching David how to operate the cart, and still, David was nervous driving it. It was not that it was a difficult piece of machinery, but the custom Garia cart—which was street legal according to the doctor—would set David back over seventy grand if he wrecked it.

He had, to no avail, tried to use his car. However, Dr. Neil assured him that if he did, he would get some stares. No one drove cars in Havana except when they arrived and when they left. The roads were too narrow and the town too small. David ultimately caved while in his mind calculating how many lectures he would have to agree to if he damaged the cart.

Right at eight Bella stepped from the front door of the diner. She had ditched the blue and white striped dress and white apron for a pair of jean shorts and a tank top. Her hair had gone from a bun to hanging freely from her scalp, carefully laid over her left shoulder.

"You made it," she said smiling as she slid into the passenger seat. "I see Dr. Neil let you borrow his cart. Did he tell you what it cost?"

119

"Unfortunately," David acknowledged. "I take it he is mighty proud of the price tag."

"Part of the territory. After you spend enough time in Havana you start to see letting people know how much a possession costs are as normal as saying, 'Hello.'"

"How long have you been here?"

"Almost a decade."

"Do you live here?" David began to back the cart out of the parking spot he created near the diner.

"Oh yes, the diner's wages and the tips from customers bought me a nice shanty on the beach."

David chuckled, "I didn't know if they had dorms for people who worked here, perhaps."

"No, I live on the outside in a small apartment with my roommate. But sometimes in the off-season, I'll camp on the beach if it isn't too cold."

"Off-season?"

"Yeah, from mid-October to sometime in May most residents abandon ship. The winters aren't very fun up this far."

"What do you do for work then?" As David drove, Bella would point him to his next move. He was paying more attention to her than the road, glancing over often enough to not hit anything, but not enough to remember what direction they were going.

"Work at the Dollar Tree and take up odd jobs. One bright side to having a roommate is the rent is shared."

"How did you get on at the diner?" David asked.

"Here," Bella said pointing to his left. David turned down a narrow dirt road cautious not to let any of the overgrown branches scrape the cart. "My Aunt was a cleaning lady for Mr. Roads. He is probably the richest guy in town, and funded half of Havana's construction costs himself. She told him I was looking for work after I graduated from high school. After I came home from college with my bachelor's in criminal justice, I started working out at the diner until I decided what to do with my life." She chuckled softly, shaking her head in disbelief. "That was close to ten years ago."

"Why didn't you pursue a career in the field?"

"I thought about it. I guess when I came back that summer to work here, I grew comfortable."

David could understand that. Comfort was a powerful thing, especially when the alternative was the unknown. "Is Mr. Roads still around?"

Bella looked at him quizzically, "Yes, he should be at the diner tomorrow for breakfast. Kind of his routine. Why?"

"Just curious. I have been tinkering with investments and I would like to pick the mind of such a genius."

"Well, he is usually there by eight."

They drove for a few minutes in silence until the road ended. The narrow gravel road gave way to the expansive beach and the suffocating trees opened. A hundred yards from them was a lighthouse, about half the size of a proper one, David thought. He could just barely make out the fence a few yards beyond that. He wondered why it had been put there. It was out of the way enough that he could not imagine many people visiting the site and small enough that he doubted anyone on the water would notice it either.

"It was built to commemorate the opening of the community," she said as if reading his mind. "The light guides you home to where love awaits the weary."

David let the words sink in. The beauty filled him slowly as each word replayed in his mind. "Who wrote that?"

"Not sure, it is what the plaque on the lighthouse says. Havana is home."

"Even for you?"

Bella sat there for a moment pondering the question. She knew as much about the community as those who inhabited it. Probably more. She knew the people as intimately as their own families. In David's world, that meant it was home for her, but only if she saw it as such.

"I like to think so," she said.

As David drove Bella back to the diner, he felt tense from the silence. It was a sensation to which he was not accustomed. Half of his career was built on the power of silence. Still, at that moment, he was not comfortable. Then he wondered if he might just want to hear Bella speak.

"I noticed some deliveries coming into the dock pretty late the past couple of nights. Seems like quite the hassle."

Bella shook her head dramatically and her eyes narrowed doubtfully. "What?"

"The last couple of nights I saw a boat docked up and some people unloading it. Seemed like a lot for such a small community."

Bella did not say anything but her body language spoke clearly. "What's the matter?"

"There shouldn't be any deliveries past six. And except for a few packages, supplies and goods are brought in on Tuesdays."

"Oh," David said unsure of whether Bella was offended. "Maybe it was something else. I wasn't all that close. Mainly just saw the boat and people on the dock."

"Maybe," Bella said with a shrug. This hypothesis seemed to suit her, but David knew that whatever happened on the dock was nothing other than a delivery of some sort.

CHAPTER 20

Jack arrived at the old Ritz Theater a little after midnight. The Catacombs were of no use to him. A few users huddled in a corner lost deep in their high and a few low-end dealers booted when they saw him enter. But Cheddar was nowhere to be seen. He could care less about booking a newbie dealer for a few bags of crank or weed. He needed to find his informant.

The Ritz had at one time been a beautiful building. Even looking at the decaying structure then he could tell it had once been stunning. The three-story building looked like an old church. The dark brown bricks outlined in light masonry. An elegant 'R' that looked like the craftsman had hobbies centered in calligraphy. Two gargoyles stood guard over the building from perches at the top of the building.

The outside clearly showed wear and signs of decay, but the inside had all but lost its soul. Sections of the second and third floors had caved entirely—leaving some sections completely exposed to the elements, graffiti claimed every inch of the walls, staircases caved under invisible weight, and any charm the building once had, had long since gone.

Fewer people were calling it home than some would suspect. There were better places in town for squatters to find refuge for a night. Places with roofs and less concern of a floor falling in on them. However, this was exactly why Cheddar liked to hang low here when he needed to. No one thought to come around and look for him there. No one except Jack.

Jack went around to the back of the building and found the window with the wooden board covering it. The one that just sat on the sill and was not nailed down. He slid it off to the side and climbed into the open window, hoping he would not land on a used needle or spook someone into attacking him. While he was climbing, he would be vulnerable and ill-prepared to defend himself.

Fortunately, Jack made it inside without incident. He pulled his flashlight from his hip and let the radiant white beam show him the room. It was empty and looked as though no one had been using it for recreation. He continued out into the hall and turned right towards what had once been the lobby of the theater. Jack transitioned the flashlight from his right to his left hand, then placed the butt of his right hand on the grip of his Glock 17.

He called out to Cheddar, but not so loudly as to startle anything or anyone inside. Just a low call as he might do if he were calling a dog in from outside.

When he reached the atrium, he found it empty. He explored the old lobby for a few minutes. Jack continued to call out gently to Cheddar but noticed each time he did his frustrations grew and it reflected in his voice.

He did not know if Cheddar had wandered off to the second or third floor, but if he had, Jack would not be finding out. The structure was too unsound to risk it, and unlike Cheddar, he cared what happened to him.

Jack let his right-hand fall from the butt of his pistol and spun around slowly one more time, letting the beam of light guide his eyes to anything that appeared out of the regular. Then he spotted something.

In the center of the room, a piece of plywood—which looked like it had fallen from the ceiling above the spot—leaned against a concrete beam. It appeared out of place to him. If the wood had fallen from the floor above it would have landed flat on the ground. If someone had moved it, they had a reason. Most likely, trying to conceal something, or themselves, he thought.

Jack put his hand back on the gun and approached the leaning piece of wood slowly, cautious to not make much noise. When he stood two feet from the board, he kicked it simultaneously drawing his weapon. As the board rocked against the concrete pillar, he noticed a pair of shoes tucked behind the wood.

"Get out here, right now!" He demanded, the booming of his command knocking dust free from all around him.

Nothing.

"I won't tell you a third time, pal. Get the fuck out right now, or I will make you get out!"

Nothing.

Jack kicked the right side of the board and let it spin free from the pillar. As he expected someone was there, and as he hoped, it was Cheddar. What he did not expect was to find him dead with a fresh bullet hole in his right temple.

CHAPTER 21

David woke the next morning ten minutes before his alarm. His mind had been able to find rest after his evening with Bella. His thoughts shifted from the strange man in the Baker's home to Bella's lips. On her eyes. And her flowing hair. He thought about how full of life she was and how inspired he felt by her optimistic views on life.

He dressed for the day and while his main objective was to meet and speak to Mr. Roads, he found himself thinking more of Bella than the mogul. He did a short meditation and then stood in the sand of the backyard for a few minutes. He closed his eyes and allowed himself to be completely present to the sun soaking into his flesh. He tried to shift all focus to only the things around him—the sound of the birds, and the lake crashing into the sand, the feeling of the sun, the smell of the water—but his mind kept returning to Bella.

He had not thought about a woman this intimately since Alice, he realized. Could that be? He had dated quite a bit since college, but nothing ever went much further than that, despite his mother's pleas for a daughter-in-law and a house full of grandchildren. He had never found a woman that struck him like Alice had, at least, not until now.

Suddenly he felt regret and sadness tugging at him like a jockey pulling the reigns of his horse. The regret of Alice had served as an anchor in his life, keeping him stuck where he was and not allowing him to drift.

David shook the thoughts from his mind and took one more deep breath before he headed for the cart. He would drop it off at Dr. Neil's on his way back from the diner and figure something else out if he needed.

Even at 7:30 a.m., the humidity had grown heavy. He felt sticky in his breathable polo shirt and golf shorts. The label had claimed to be moisture-wicking and cooling when he bought them but now seemed to hold onto every drop of sweat and moisture stuck in the air. He hoped that he would dry out on the ride to the diner, but in those fifteen minutes, he also feared he would only sweat more. He did not know if it had to do with the lake or if Indiana was amid a harsh heatwave. Either way, it was unpleasant. He decided he would swim in the lake later in the day before trying to call Jack again.

Fifteen minutes later he was at the diner and finding sanction in the AC which blasted his flesh upon entry. Goosebumps rose on his arms and he shivered twice, but it felt lovely. Bella noticed him from behind the counter and a wide smile illuminated her face. He could not help but smile back.

She disappeared for a moment and then reappeared from the hallway. "Glad you could make it," she said as she neared him.

"Of course." She took his hand and lead him to one of the six stools at the counter. He had not noticed them the day before, but he did not look that hard, either.

"You can sit here. Mr. Roads always sits there," she pointed two stools down from his. "Same one every time. I figured it would make it less awkward if you were close rather than having to walk up to him."

"I appreciate that. Do you think he will talk to an outsider? Especially about financial advice?"

Bella shrugged. "Hard to tell. Sometimes he is warm and welcoming and sometimes he seems standoffish." She brushed his arm with her hand. "Just let him have a few sips of his coffee first."

David chuckled, "Great advice."

David sat at his stool and Bella vanished back into the hall. She returned in front of him on the other side of the counter. "What kind of breakfast guy are you," she asked. David thought there was a playfulness in her voice, but he did not want to overthink it.

"What do you mean?"

"Greasy and delicious or healthy and boring?"

"I take it you are more of the former?"

"Guilty."

David smiled, "It is vacation. I guess I can live a little. I will take something greasy and delicious."

"Good choice," she said with a smile. "Coffee?"

"Please."

David turned in his stool and scanned the diner. There were five tables with people filling their bellies for the day. The table directly in front of him held three men, two well into their sixties. Two of them had heads as gray as ash and the third longed for even a strand of their gray locks. The men all wore tacky Hawaiian shirts which resembled Dr. Neil's. He wondered what the fascination was amongst the old men in Havana with these gaudy pieces of clothing. David recognized the men from the doctor's party, one being the man who seemed put off by David.

At another table was a young family. The parents were about his age. The father wore a monogrammed shirt with a skateboard on it and some basketball shorts. He had thick glasses which magnified his eyes to alien proportions. The man's wife was beautiful with long golden hair tied into a bun at the pinnacle of her scalp. She wore a white tank top and cutoff shorts. Their daughter resembled the mother but had been born with her father's poor eyesight. Though her glasses were not as thick, they were the largest he had seen on any child of eight years old.

Before David could inspect the other patrons, he heard the door open. A man of about forty walked in and his stature seemed to demand respect, if everyone did not honor his entrance, it felt like a major offense. The man wore a full sleeve button-down and white slacks, despite the heat he appeared unfazed. His black hair was partially concealed behind a tennis visor. He stood at the door for only a second before heading towards the counter.

"Good morning, Mr. Roads," Bella said from the register.

David had wondered if this man was Mr. Roads when he entered. He was younger than David imagined. He had envisioned an old man who had worked his entire life never getting enough recognition. Leading him to build an elite community in which he would live on forever, honored and loved. But this man was much younger and more vibrant than the man he had imagined. Mr. Roads would have been in his early thirties when Havana had been constructed. David was impressed.

Mr. Roads sat at the seat Bella said he would. His butt barely touched the brown leather of the seat before Bella slid a steaming cup of coffee and a plate of French toast in front of him. One minute before she brought David his order.

David had been nibbling at his food for a few minutes when he looked up at Bella. She nodded in Mr. Roads' direction with encouragement in her eyes.

"Sure, is hot out there," David said.

Mr. Roads remained silent. It was as if David had said nothing at all.

David took a swig from his coffee and smacked his lips together twice. "It's not Saint Helena Coffee, but it's good."

This caught Mr. Roads' attention. He looked up from his nearly empty plate. "A connoisseur?"

David chuckled, "Oh, hardly. I just appreciate the finer experiences in life. Why should a good cup of coffee be any different?"

"You haven't known the true pleasure of coffee until you have had Black Ivory."

David smiled. He had spent a month in Thailand before heading off to his master's program. He had gone with two of his college buddies as their last great ride. They had split the sixty-dollar cup of coffee. The barista made it a point to let them know how fortunate they were to have gotten the cup because it was such a rare bean. "I enjoy the sweet hint of chocolate and the subtleness of the spices. The tea-like consistency makes it more unique than just any other cup of coffee."

At this, Mr. Roads leaned back in his stool. His face showcased how impressed he was, "I work with some of the richest men in the world who have not had such fortune. How did you happen to find such luck?"

"Right place, right time. Kind of the story of my life."

Mr. Roads tapped the stool next to him. David stood from his seat and walked the three steps to the one beside Mr. Roads and sat down.

"I have never seen you around here. I don't recall any property coming up for sale, either. I am on the zoning commission," he said with a smug smile.

"I do not own property. I am visiting for the week."

His impressed look faded to one of distrust, "I see." He returned his focus to the plate in front of him.

David pretended not to notice, "I figured if I was going to move, I should experience it first. I thought this week would tell me everything I needed to know about Havana and if I wanted to move here if something opened."

"I have a feeling something will be open very soon," he said. His eyes were still on his plate and his voice lacked interest.

"So, how did you find yourself on the zoning board?" David knew that a man like Mr. Roads loved nothing more than an opportunity to talk about himself. This time was no different.

Mr. Roads' eyes met David's and a self-satisfied smile crept onto his face, widening as he spoke, "I'm the unofficial Mayor of Havana. I funded ninety percent of the costs to build it and so I have a say in anything that happens here. That includes what is built and who moves in."

"That is impressive! You must be one helluva businessman to be able to fund all of this."

Mr. Roads nodded, his smirk now threatening to stretch his face beyond its normal ability. "I have had a lot of luck in the stock market and have always been fortunate in business. Leased my first business property at twenty. Made six hundred million before I was thirty."

"Jesus, that is remarkable. I thought I made a good living as a therapist." David tapped the table as if thinking. "You know, I have had nothing but failing luck on stocks. Any advice you can give me?"

"Go with start-ups in growing fields. Everyone will tell you to go with established companies and all of that, but it's bull shit. Cost too much to get to a point where it matters and your returns aren't for shit. Buy cheap and sell high."

"You know, I ran into a couple whom I think visited here once, the Baker's. They told me import and export was how to build a solid fortune."

Mr. Roads' eyes narrowed. He cleared his throat before speaking. "Yes, Braden and Caroline. They own a house in Havana. Word of advice, mister..."

"David. You can call me David."

"Braden is a fucking idiot. You would be wise not to take advice from that fool."

David tried to smile as if amused by the comment. He was unsure if he was convincing or not, but he had spent his entire career concealing his thoughts through his facial reactions. "I got that vibe from him, myself."

"Well, it was nice to meet you, David." Mr. Roads stood from his stool and tossed a hundred-dollar bill on the countertop. He turned to leave, and David racked his brain looking for a way to keep him there to see if Braden and Caroline had been to Havana recently. But then Mr. Roads stopped. In a fluent glide of his hand, he retrieved a card from his breast pocket and slid it in front of David. "I am going golfing with a few investors tomorrow. You should join us." Then he left.

Bella came over as soon as the door closed behind Mr. Roads. "How was it? Did you get any wise investment tips?"

"Maybe. Not sure yet," David said watching Mr. Roads enter his own cart and then drive off in the direction opposite of his rental property. "Hey," he said turning to Bella. "Do you get a lunch break?"

"I am off at one. Why?"

"Want to go for a swim?"

CHAPTER 22

David browsed the paperback section of the bookstore until one. There were no options he felt would suitably fill any downtime he might have. They were all the same romance novels his aunt used to read. Books of lustful affairs but little substance. Essentially, the same content as the mindless sludge from the dating shows on TV.

There had been a few magazines he flipped through, but again, nothing he felt would do him much good in trying to kill time. He knew, though, that his time in Havana was growing shorter and he doubted there would be much downtime at all. Not if he hoped to figure out where Caroline and Braden had gone. At the very least, figure out why they felt the need to disappear.

As David left the bookstore, he slid his hand into his right pocket and felt the card Mr. Roads had given him. He would call him that night and go to the golf outing. Someone there might know something, and while he would not ask them outright, he figured he could gauge whether they had seen his clients recently. He would wade those waters carefully and strategically. He also thought, if he were there, he may be able to point out the man who had broken into the house after him. The breathing and heavy footfalls would be a dead giveaway.

David stood outside of the diner for only a minute before Bella emerged. She had changed into a pair of shorts that rode high on her tan legs and a deep purple tank top.

"Lucky for me I didn't do laundry yet. I have a spare set of clothes."

"That is lucky," David agreed. "No cart today. Do you want to take your car?"

"Actually, my roommate dropped me off. I just called to let her know I will call her when I am done." Bella followed David as he began walking back towards his rental.

"That is a nice roommate. I only had roommates in college, but I know none of them would have been so gracious with their transporting services."

Bella chuckled, "Janice works from home. Driving me to and from work is the most she gets out so she looks forward to it."

"Yeah, I did telehealth for a while during the pandemic. It was nice, but I like being part of the world. Not just another face on the screen."

"I don't think I could work from home. I like people too much."

"I get that," David told her. As they walked her hand brushed against his, then again. A moment later, their fingers were tied together.

"I love hearing people's stories and feeling like I am a part of their lives."

"You are part of their lives. For some people, you may be the only part of their day they have to look forward to."

"Most of the people I see are rich beyond measure. I am certain I am not the highlight of their day. The rich are not that lonely."

"Definitely the rich," David told her.

She looked at him quizzically, gauging whether he was serious.

"My practice is made up entirely of wealthy people. I always operate at full capacity and turn people away weekly. I speak at conferences four times a year and at least half of the audience would be considered wealthy. Money doesn't buy good company."

When they reached the house, they walked right around to the back and down the beach. The sand was hot as it seeped into David's sandals. They picked up their pace until they reached where the waves had soaked the sand, making it more tolerable.

David removed his sandals, shirt, and belongings from his pocket, tossing them to the sand.

Bella removed her tank top revealing a matching sports bra.

"Last one in makes dinner," David shouted as he broke for the water. Bella grabbed his arm and pulled him back even with her. David slowed a step allowing her to dive into the water just feet ahead of him.

"I hope you're a good cook," she said after she emerged from the water.

David walked into the water standing beside her. He watched the water glisten on her skin and drip from her hair, making rhythmic trickles when it hit the lake. "Terrible," he told her.

She took a step towards David and he wrapped his arms around her waist. His heart began to pound in his chest so hard he felt as though his ribs would separate. The thudding traveled into his back. He had not felt this close to a woman in some time. It was foreign to him.

"That's too bad," she said, allowing her body to go closer to his.

David put his right hand on her cheek and pulled her face towards his, kissing her deeply.

David showed Bella the dryer and gave her a towel, then led her to the shower. He left her in private and headed down to the kitchen. The promise of dinner was a tactic he had not fully thought out.

He had made the bet and allowed her to win so that he could spend more time with her. However, he had not considered the fact he did not have much food in the house. At least nothing suitable for a dinner.

He called Dr. Neil and gave him a quick rundown of his plight. Before David finished telling Dr. Neil he needed help, there was a knock on his front door. It was so gentle he hardly heard it at all.

David opened the door to three tote bags on the porch. Dr. Neil was in his cart giving David two thumbs up, beaming as a father might when his son hits his first home run. He gathered the bags and waved to the doctor before rushing back into the kitchen.

David unloaded the bags and stood amazed at what the doctor had provided. A whole duck, two large potatoes, a bag of brussels sprouts, olive oil, and one whole bag of seasonings and dried spices. A rush of overwhelm hit him.

He turned to check the time, feeling some relief to see it was only three in the afternoon. He set his oven to Three-fifty and began organizing the contents on his counter. He heard the shower turn off upstairs, he decided to call Mr. Roads before Bella came down.

The phone rang twice, "Mr. Roads, speaking."

"Hello, Mr. Roads. This is David, we met this morning at the diner. I would love to take you up on that offer. I must let you know, I did not bring any clubs, though. I hope that is not an issue."

"Good to hear. And not at all, there is always a spare set or two at the clubhouse for guests. I will pick you up at eight-thirty, sharp. Be ready." And with that, Mr. Roads hung up

"Oh, wow!" Bella's voice caused David to spin around, slightly startled. "You know when I said, 'I hope you can cook' I was only kidding. I was thinking something like pasta or burgers."

"I don't get to cook for others that often. I take advantage when I can." David looked at the oven. "It will take about three hours. Is that too long?"

"Not at all," she told him, tying her hair up behind her head. "Just means you have to put up with me for a while longer," she walked up to him and put her head on his chest. He kissed the crown of her head.

"That's a price I will gladly pay."

"How far is Indianapolis from here?"

"Three hours or so." David knew why she was asking. In a couple of days, he would have to go back home. Where would that leave her? Where would that leave them? David pulled away from her.

"I haven't been totally honest with you," he said. "About why I am here."

A look of concern spread across Bella's face. "You're not on the run from the law, are you?"

David smiled, "No. At least not yet."

"What's up?" Bella lifted herself onto the counter and sat there, her eyes trained on David.

"Would you like some wine?"

"A wine secret. Must be serious."

David retrieved a bottle and two glasses. He took his time filling them, creating the proper wording in his mind. He did not want Bella to think he was crazy, obsessive, or anything negative. David wanted her to think of him as she did now, and nothing less.

When the wine was poured, he leaned his hip against the oven and told her why he had come to Havana.

CHAPTER 23

"Who would have known to check for the ledger besides you?" He demanded answers from the figure, but it had none.

"Someone who knew what was inside. Are there any other leaks in the pipeline?"

He thought for a moment. No one else was as stupid as Braden. Everyone else knew to keep their fucking mouths shut and they knew not to threaten him. They knew the consequences of such foolishness. "No," he answered. "But I want you to find out who has the ledger. I want their head on my desk by the end of the week."

⚜

Bella had reacted to the news better than David expected. He did not know how, exactly, he expected her to react, but he knew how crazy it sounded. A therapist going across the state to track down a client who missed one session. Perhaps it was the concern that his client's husband had something to do with it that provided Bella more sympathy than concern.

"And you cannot tell me who it is? I might be able to help."

"I can't. I really shouldn't have told you what I did."

Bella held David's hand in hers. "And you think Mr. Roads had something to do with it, now?"

David shook his head. "I don't know that. I just think a man with as much power as he has in this community... if anyone knows something he will. I don't even know how I would get that information from him if he does."

"He certainly has a mean streak. I don't think it is that far outside the realm of possibility that if he felt crossed in some way, he would handle someone."

"I just don't get it." David shook his head as if doing so would allow the pieces to fall into place within his mind. "What could be so important he would want them out of the picture? And if it were my client's husband, why wouldn't he have done more to cover his tracks?"

"What do you mean?"

"Like not calling her into work or canceling the session with me. He just disappeared right along with her. That's not very smart."

"You said the police were going to be following up back home, right? Yesterday or today? Have you heard anything about it?"

"No. My buddy Jack who is a detective said he would keep me updated. But it isn't his department and I am sure he is swamped. He has not returned my calls which only happens when the paperwork is higher than his desk."

"My dad was a cop. I get it."

"Promise me you will not mention anything to anyone else. Not at the diner, not around Havana, not even to your roommate."

"I won't. Your secret is safe with me." She pulled herself into him, wrapping his arms around her as she did so. "Just make sure you stay safe."

"I will. I will go golf with Mr. Roads tomorrow and if nothing pans out from that, I will let the police handle it."

"Are you a good golfer?"

"Define good," David said with a chuckle. "It doesn't matter. The answer is no."

CHAPTER 24

David woke up shortly before 6 a.m. His back was stiff from having slept on the couch. He let Bella take the bed. As much as he wanted to sleep with her the night before, he respected her, and he was an old soul when it came to chivalry. He wanted her to know that he wanted more than just her body. He wanted her time and her energy, he wanted her conversation, he wanted all of her.

David wondered if he should question his own sanity. He had not been acting rationally. Traveling across the state to find a client, sneaking into both of her homes, and now falling in love, or at least deep infatuation, with a woman he had just met. None of this was David. It was all out of character for him.

He started a pot of coffee and left a cup out for her. Then he took a quick shower in the downstairs bathroom and put on a polo shirt and a pair of khakis he had packed. He wished he had brought more shorts, knowing that the heat of the day would be as unrelenting as it had been all week. At 8:20 a.m., he went upstairs and kissed Bella on the forehead. Then, he went outside to wait for Mr. Roads.

As soon as he closed the front door, Mr. Roads was pulling up in a cart just as nice as Dr. Neil's. The man was punctual if nothing else. After glancing at his watch, David saw he technically had five minutes to spare. He sped-walked to the cart feeling as though Mr. Roads was a man whose time was precious.

Once in the passenger seat, Mr. Roads gave David a firm shake. He was wearing a thin pair of white shorts and a dark blue Rhoback shirt.

David did not wait long to spark conversation. While he was accustomed to silence, he did not want Mr. Roads to spend too much time in his mind or to become comfortable in their silence. If he did, David knew, it would be much harder to get him to open up later. Especially with others around. "Does Havana have a private golf course?"

"Not technically. It has a private entrance to one, but the course is pretty exclusive. If Havana were not here, neither would it. So, I guess in a way, it is our private course."

"You said you were meeting investors? New business venture?

Mr. Roads laughed mockingly, "I have plenty of businesses Mr. Thorne. They are just some old friends who get whimsical ideas as most fools do. We get together every few months for a few beers and a few holes, they pitch me ridiculous ideas, and I will front them some start-up money."

David forced himself to appear impressed. "Seems like you have hit more than you've lost."

Mr. Roads shook his head. "I rarely request a stake in their ventures. But I can write it off, so I figure no harm, no foul." Mr. Roads gripped the wheel tightly and rotated his hands around it. "Besides, my father always said, 'when you are wealthy it is good to help your friends. You never know when you might need their help.' So, I front some cash. Plenty more to be found."

"Your father sounds like a decent man."

"He had his moments. My brother reminds me a lot of him."

David noticed a change in his voice. It lowered and slowed in tempo as if he were getting lost in a memory. He decided to switch gears, "I guess it comes with the territory."

"What's that?"

"Success and moochers. Like gnats to a light."

Mr. Roads let out a roaring laugh that bellowed deep from his throat. "That's the fucking truth."

"Are you and your brother close," David asked.

"No," Roads said with pain in his voice. David decided to leave it alone.

"I remember after I started my practice no one spread the word. No one referred anyone to me. After I rented a penthouse and bought a Jag, everyone wanted something. A loan here, start-up there, advice on business."

"Leeches have more scruples than people. They do not hide the fact they are trying to suck you dry and take everything you are worth. People will try to play you so long as you let them."

David faked a laugh as if a funny story popped into his mind. He apologized and Mr. Roads requested—in a demanding undertone—that he be filled in. "Just reminds me of a guy I know. Visited, or lives here, actually. In Havana. The guy I mentioned yesterday, Braden. He asked me at some event to invest in something he was starting up. Told him to kick rocks."

Mr. Roads did not mimic David's fake laugh. Instead, his hands tightened more on the wheel and he looked at David quizzically. Then he returned his eyes to the road. "You said you're a therapist, right?"

"Yes." David felt himself grow nervous. He wondered how much Mr. Roads hated the Bakers. David guessed a man of his wealth could make anyone disappear.

"Wasn't Caroline in therapy?"

David shook his head. "Wouldn't know. I did not know them all that well. As I said they were at an event and he approached me about the investment. After I told him I was not interested his wife came up and the conversation about Havana came up."

"What did they have to say about it? That's not privileged, is it?"

David forced another laugh. He feared his nervousness soaking through. "No worries there, Mr. Roads. That only applies to clients. They just said it was a beautiful place and perfect for self-care."

"I see."

"Did I offend you? You seem pretty upset just at the name of them."

Mr. Roads seemed to flip a switch. His hands loosened and became relaxed on the wheel, he even allowed his body to lean back lazily into the seat. A smile crept across his cheeks, "One of those bad investments I made."

"Then I am glad I dodged that bullet."

Mr. Roads turned to David, his smile widening which narrowed his eyes. "It was a big bullet."

The words sent a chill through David's spine.

The golf course required they drive the cart across the beach, past the lighthouse, and along the shore a quarter of a mile until they reached a point where the gate opened to asphalt. The rear of the clubhouse looked like a large hunting cabin. The whole building was made of thick logs with a wraparound porch set up with white rocking chairs.

Carts sat in a nice line down the front of the building. David could see little flags scattered around the wide expanse. Small rolling hills strategically placed between miniature ponds and sand pits. Trees had been planted in such a way that a half foot off and the golfer would be searching thick grass for his ball rather than the fairway.

The two parked in front of a group of four men. They all appeared to be in their forties. Three of them almost looked like triplets, though clearly, were not. All three appeared to be at least thirty pounds overweight, each wore fashionable glasses, and all three were balding from their scalp. It was almost comical to David. The fourth was tall and lanky with unkempt hair and his shirt looked at least one size too big.

"Roads!" One of them shouted, clearly already having had a head start on the drinking.

"Frank, good to see you." Mr. Roads shook his hand and then turned to David. "This is David Thorne. He is my plus one, he is a guest at Havana and good company." He then swept his hand from left to right. "This is Frank. He runs a restaurant chain. Calvin owns some car dealerships, keep an eye on him. He will steal your last dollar and then ask you for change. Brice," he said pointing to the third man. "Brice is a serial entrepreneur who is a successful seller of some useless crap online."

"Hey, I run a reputable business," Brice's words were serious, but his smile hinted he was not. He reminded David of a child telling his father a fib and finding pleasure in thinking he was getting one over on his old man.

Mr. Roads threw out a groan and a laugh that bled together oddly, "And that is Clive, he was a lawyer who somehow got his mega-millionaire client to leave him everything upon his passing."

"Just a fortunate case of right-place-right-time," Clive said with a grin.

"Who brought the cigars?" Mr. Roads scanned the small group waiting for a response.

"That would be me," Frank said pulling five fat brown rolls from his breast pocket. A Zippo emerged from the same pocket once everyone had their cigar in hand, ends already clipped.

"Is that cedar I smell?" David asked.

"Good nose," Frank said. "Got them from a guy I know. The best cigar you will ever taste."

"They are Cubans," Clive added. "He gets them from a bodega in Florida from a Cuban guy. He just asks for the most expensive ones he has. Don't let the smell fool you, usually smell great, and tastes like dog shit."

Mr. Roads laughed, "At least he didn't bring those Swishers. Should have banned you for life for that one."

"I forgot it was my turn. In case you hadn't noticed, the shit-hole that surrounds this little paradise doesn't have much in terms of a high-class establishment."

"Let's get moving. I am interested to hear what you fellas have to try and sell me on today."

The group split. Mr. Roads, David, and Calvin got into one cart while Frank, Brice and Clive got into the other. "You can use Clive's clubs today," Mr. Roads said to David.

"Excuse me?" Clive said from behind the wheel of his cart. He had heard Mr. Roads. He was just wanting to showcase his contempt at the sacrifice of his clubs.

"For those Swishers. I forgot how much it pissed me off."

The first three holes went well. David was last, but only by two strokes. Mr. Roads was in the lead, ahead by four strokes. But he noticed the other four men would, at times, intentionally foul up a shot to add strokes. He thought it may be to stroke Mr. Roads' ego and to put him in a better mood for their sale. But there was also something about the way the men interacted with him. As if they feared him.

On the fifth hole, Clive started the spiel, "You know it's great being rich," he said.

"Amen to that," Mr. Roads said as he slid a wood driver into its place in the bag.

"But not many people get to enjoy the luxury," Frank chimed.

"What if they could," Calvin rounded. "What if everyone could be rich? At least, for a day or two?"

Mr. Roads looked at them as if they spoke a language he had never heard before. He turned his ear closer to them as if doing so would make their words clearer.

"What if people could buy a *rich-cation*, working title, of course."

"Yes, they buy a two-day package where they get to live the life of a millionaire. Live in their home, use their drivers, and have a night on the town, as if they are the millionaire."

Mr. Roads chuckled amused. He looked at David and pointed at the four men with his thumb. "Didn't I tell you?"

He turned his attention to Frank, Clive, Brice, and Calvin. Frank spoke, "We would like you to be one of the options. The 'exclusive package'." Frank said, continuing valiantly at peaking Mr. Roads' ego.

"That is the stupidest fucking idea I think I have ever heard." Mr. Roads' tone was even and blunt. The four men tensed up as if about to be struck, but David could not find anger in his voice. "Let me tell you something, anyone who could afford to pay the cost that any millionaire would be willing to allow a stranger to have access to their life, is just well enough off to be content. Those who would do anything to have that experience, would not be able to afford it. And those in the middle, no one would trust with their things."

"Right, which is why we do it virtually," Clive said in an apologetic tone.

"Yes, VR. It is affordable for everyone and the entire experience is in virtual reality," Calvin said, sounding slightly more confident than Clive.

Mr. Road's face dove into contemplation. Numbers crunching in his head and marketing ideas flying past like snapshots on a reel. He was growing intrigued. "Go on."

Frank smiled a hopeful smile, "What does it cost for two nights in the Ritz? To rent a car? To dine at one of the finest establishments in New York? You are talking thousands."

"By doing it in VR, they can live that experience for under two grand," Clive said. "And the best part," he continued before Mr. Roads could interject, "the rich who grant access to their homes, cars, and likeness will be granted 40% of the revenue earned in their life experience."

Mr. Roads looked at David, "Care to chime in?"

David shook his head, unsure of what he could offer. He loathed technology and had seen it devastate many lives and relationships. Granting such a realistic experience to people who were looking for an escape seemed dangerous to him. Pulling them further from reality and making their ability to cope with their real problems that much more challenging. "I am afraid I fall into the 'content' category."

"How much do you make per year?" Mr. Roads asked bluntly.

"Pardon me?"

"I need to know who the demographic would be. If you are content, others in your tax bracket will be too. Obviously, you are not the ideal client. So, what do you make?"

David threw out a ballpark number a little lower than his actual income. "Around five-hundred-thousand, I suppose."

"Before taxes?" Frank asked, making David more uncomfortable.

"Yes," he lied.

"Okay, so that doesn't help. You are part of the one-percent everyone hates. What does the start-up cost?"

David watched the men discuss this plan for another hour, waiving other golfers around them as they spoke. After an hour and a half of talking, Mr. Roads denied the deal. There was a sense of pleasure in it for him, strong enough that one could taste it.

"It is a good idea," he said. "But you do not have enough yet. Get it ironed out and bring it back to me in two months.

The men played two more holes before heading to the clubhouse to begin drinking.

CHAPTER 25

Clive excused himself to go to the restroom. He was six beers in and the way he had been bouncing his knee, David was surprised he had not already pissed himself. David waited a minute before checking his phone and excusing himself. He wanted to speak with Clive. Alone. Clive seemed like the most vulnerable in the group, the least loyal. If anyone had something to say about Mr. Roads, David thought it would be him.

Clive was coming out of the restroom pulling a cigarette from its golden pack. He seemed startled when he almost ran into David.

"Excuse me," David said, "I was just going to step outside and send an e-mail."

"I'll join you," he said. "Need a few puffs anyway."

When the two were outside David began typing on his phone as if sending his correspondence. Clive sparked his cigarette and took a long hard drag on it, exhaling the thick white cloud and taking with it, his sense of tension.

"That was some impressive work," David said through feverish typing, never letting his eyes leave his screen.

"What was?"

"The way you four worked Mr. Roads. I have never seen anything like it. It was impressive." David looked at Clive to show he meant what he said and was not being sardonic.

"If only it worked," Clive said with his cigarette dangling from his lips.

"Seemed like it worked. Didn't he say to bring it back to him?"

Clive nodded with a smile. "Which to him means, no. The other guys have sold him on other businesses in the past. This was my first attempt, but I think it holds promise."

"I do too. It's the safer version of *Total Recall*."

A light went off in the man's head. "Not just the rich, but a vacation in the life of a spy or a secret agent. That's genius."

"Maybe in the next meeting, you can bring that up."

"There won't be one. The others will move on to the next idea entirely and I don't have the pull with Mr. Roads to seek funding from him to go at it alone."

Clive seemed to have more confidence on the golf course. When he was talking about the business idea his head was high and he spoke with direction. Now, his head hung and he pulled at the cigarette as if it would run from his lungs. David did not know if he was defeated or if he were drunk. Probably a mixture of both.

"You could go at it alone," David offered.

"Mr. Roads doesn't like people coming to him with business. The only reason he allows it here is that we all go back a way. And since I know Frank and Brice, by next time they will have their new idea ready to pitch to him."

"What if you beat them to the punch and brought it back up?"

Clive shot him a serious look, "You do not do that. If he does not bite the first time, it is dead in the water. Bring it up again and you have to deal with the consequences."

David let out a chuckle, "Like what? Not getting funded the next time?"

Clive widened his eyes and shook his head slowly. "It gets a lot uglier than that. Trust me. Mr. Roads isn't someone you want to piss off. Not if you like being healthy."

"Fellas!" Frank shouted stumbling out of the clubhouse, Brice, and Mr. Roads just behind him. Calvin remained inside talking to a young female server. "Why didn't you tell us the party moved out here?"

"I just had to reply to an e-mail," David said, shaking his phone at Frank before sliding it into his pocket.

Clive put the cigarette out in the ashtray beside him and stood up. "I needed a few puffs."

"Well, Brice and I must go. Early meeting tomorrow. Are you coming along, Clive?"

"Yes."

The men all shook hands and said their goodbyes. Frank said he would be in contact with Mr. Roads in a day or two, which Mr. Roads nodded approval for. The men began crossing the parking lot and Calvin burst from the door in chase. Once they vanished across the parking lot, Mr. Roads stepped up to stand directly beside David.

"What were you two talking about?"

"Oh," David was a little surprised by the sudden interrogation. At least, that is how it sounded with Mr. Roads' tone. "Nothing. Just told him I thought the business idea was clever and how impressed I was with the presentation. I do not get to see things like that too often given my line of…"

"That's why I am me and you are you," Mr. Roads interrupted. "Foresight. Foresight in the outcome of a product and foresight for the people with whom you are dealing." Mr. Roads began walking away from David, a few steps away he shouted, "I'll give you a ride back to your rental."

The ride back was filled with uncomfortable silence. David was having a hard time getting a read on Mr. Roads, which was completely foreign to him. Reading people was part of his business. Part of what made him so successful. People's words can be deceiving, and even their actions can be manipulative, but their body language always told the truth. Their eyes and facial expressions told the story the rest of them would not. That was because those subtle things in body language were done unconsciously, without any thought. Most people do not consider them at all. But Mr. Roads' expressions held no clue and his eyes were blank.

When Mr. Roads stopped, he did not speak. So, as David exited the cart he stopped and stuck his hand back for a shake. "Mr. Roads it was a real pleasure. Thank you for allowing me to tag along. I enjoyed it."

Mr. Roads turned his head slowly, and like David, tried to get a read. Whatever he was looking for, he found. He shook David's hand and told him that he would see him around and to enjoy the rest of his trip.

The cart pulled away and less than ten seconds later, Dr. Neil came rolling along in his. He barely let the cart get to a complete stop before jumping out of it.

"You make a new friend?" He asked.

"Just played some golf. I met him at the diner yesterday during breakfast."

"And you made it back alive?" Dr. Neil made an expression overselling the fact he was impressed.

"What is that supposed to mean?" David was genuinely curious about Dr. Neil's remarks. He was not offended by the comment. Rather, he was intrigued. That was the second person who hinted Mr. Roads tended toward violence. Or, at least, they thought he did.

"He has this habit of being nice and generous to people in public—expressly visitors—because he is sort of the face of Havana. But that jackass is a mean and salty son-of-a-bitch. I try to avoid him at all costs."

"Thanks for the heads-up," David said. He offered Dr. Neil a beer, but he denied it.

"I just wanted to let you know to be careful with that guy. I have a date with the ball and chain tonight."

David let the conversation soak into his mind. Mr. Roads seemed like a man with a mean streak, but he did not see the man as dangerous. More like the kind of man with a fragile ego who would belittle someone to make himself feel more powerful. To show his power off to those who feared him, but nothing more.

David put his wallet on the island in the kitchen and grabbed a cold bottle of water. He began to open it when his phone rang. He let out a gentle grunt and replaced the bottle in his hand with his phone from his pocket.

"Hello, Mother. How is everything on the home front?"

"Good, as usual," she told him. "A few new clients lined up two weeks out. But that isn't why I called."

David could sense the tension in her voice. "Okay."

"I finally got a hold of someone from IMPD. No one has heard from Caroline or Braden and the police had had no luck contacting them either. They have officially opened an investigation."

David felt his stomach tighten. While he was glad the police were looking into the situation, it confirmed that something had happened to them. "When did you learn all of this?"

"Just yesterday." There was a brief pause before she spoke again. "You should head home and let them deal with this. You've done all you can."

"I cannot, Mother. Not yet."

CHAPTER 26

The previous day, Jack had received a tip that a witness spotted a white male in his early 20s fleeing from the theater shortly after 4 p.m. The witness heard two loud bangs—which was how many times Cheddar had been shot—followed by what sounded like the building collapsing, and then the white male in a black hoodie and blue jeans fleeing. The witness stated he jumped into a white Cadilac and sped away.

Nearly twenty-four hours later after working closely with vice they had three possible leads. The most likely was a local low-end dealer from a cheap rent crew working the southside. One male from the crew, Dee-Low, fit the description and was wanted on an unrelated drug charge and failure to appear.

In thirty minutes, Jack would be conducting a raid with vice, narcotics, and the SWAT team on Dee-Low's known hideout. Surveillance reported he was still there and no one else had arrived. But first, he needed to return David's calls. So, he pulled the receiver on his desk to his ear and dialed the number.

"Oh my God, he does live."

"Sorry, been a hell of a week. My snitch wound up shot last night. Not that it was needed. ME said he had OD'd on some new drug they have never seen before. But it has traces of heroin in it. Said my guy was either dead or actively dying when he was shot. Going on a bust in a bit at a stash house suspected to be pushing the stuff."

The line was silent, "Sorry, man. I didn't…"

"No shit. Don't sweat it." Jack looked up at the clock to check his time. He had ten minutes on the phone before he had to mount up. "I just wanted to return your call."

"I found a ledger in my client's house. Has a bunch of initials and prices, it was hidden in his desk."

"Drug ledger," Jack said flatly.

"That would explain the guy, then."

Jack perked at his desk, "What guy?"

"When I was in there someone else broke in and was looking for something. I only assumed it was the ledger I found."

"Goddamn, you should have called me! You need to get out of there, David. If you have something someone wants, who has already made two people disappear, you are not safe there."

"It's okay, they did not know I was there. I have been laying low… By the way," Jack could hear the smirk through the phone, "I did call you. You just didn't answer."

"Okay, asshole. Look, put that ledger somewhere safe, and when you get back in town we'll link up."

"Sounds good."

"Hey…"

"Yeah?"

"Did you really break into the house?"

David hung up the phone and began rummaging through the fridge to find what he would make for dinner. He found a steak and some broccoli, as well as the left-over duck from the night before. Then, without warning, his mind returned to Bella. He had hoped she would still be there when he returned from golf, but she had not been. She was a busy woman, and he understood that. Still, he longed to see her.

He placed the steak on the counter and went upstairs to change into something more compatible with the humidity. He grabbed a fresh tee-shirt and exchanged his polo for the lighter garment. As he began switching into new shorts, he spotted a note on the bed. David finished dressing and ran to it like a child finding candy.

David,

I had a wonderful evening. Thank you for your hospitality. It is a shame you only have a few more days here, that we only have a few more days together. I wanted to wait for you, but my roommate needed my help moving something. If you are hungry, come see me tomorrow. I work lunch and dinner.

Bella

David laid the letter to rest on the bedside table. A smile painted on his face so broad his cheeks throbbed. Then, like an alarm blasting through the silence of the night, David's smile was cleared when a shattering scream broke his moment. It came from somewhere on the beach. Far enough away that he was surprised by its clarity. Yet, it was loud. Full of terror and torment.

David looked out of the bedroom window and could see a woman, Dr. Neil's wife, he thought, standing near the brush he had seen a couple of nights before. Looking at them now, in the light of day, he thought they were roses. But he could not tell.

Then, another piercing scream came and he knew for sure she was the source. David sprinted from his room, clearing the steps two at a time, and out of the back door. He sprinted down the beach, the sand holding him and pulling at his feet like prisoners grasping at their final chance for freedom.

By time David reached her, Dr. Neil had already arrived. He grabbed his wife by the waist and pulled her to the side. His hand cupped the back of her head as he told her it was okay, he repeated it in a gentle whisper.

David's heart was pounding in his chest and each deep breath he sucked in was humid and hot, bringing no relief, only further pain. Then, he saw what had caused Mrs. Ogletree to scream.

A decomposing man lay dead in the rose patch. Roses unlike any he had ever seen. The thorns on them were a deep, dark, full red color. He assumed they were the blood-thorn roses Dr. Neil had described. The stems looked as though they were coated in blood, but he knew they were not. The red was natural to the rose, but with the body there, he could not help but wonder.

The man's face was unrecognizable. But his watch was the opposite and David knew the man right away. Braden Baker had been killed and dumped there. He began scanning the rose patch for any signs of Caroline, but Braden was the only one there.

He turned to Dr. Neil and his wife, "You take her inside and call the police. I will stay here and make sure no one else stumbles across him."

David wondered why someone would kill a man and leave him so exposed in Havana. The body, while hidden, was not hidden so it would never be found. It was hidden so more evidence would be lost. Whoever did this was not trying to get away with murder. They were trying to send a message.

But to whom? And why?

CHAPTER 27

Jack sat in his squad car one block from the stash house. The SWAT team was behind him. They had coordinated their attack three miles away in an empty parking lot. The plan was for Jack to drive up and block the driveway so no one could barrel out of there, and the SWAT van would park itself to block the street from anyone coming or going. SWAT would break into two groups, one attacking the front of the house and the other from the rear. Narcotics would join the rear entrance team while vice would run overwatch. Jack would join the front entry team and be the third man in.

He pulled his service Glock from his holster, slightly pulled the slide back, and once confident there was a hot round in the chamber, he slid it back into his holster and stuck his left hand out of the window to give the signal. He slammed on the gas. The sound of squealing tires brought him the happiness he had tried dozens of times to explain, but could never get just right.

His lightweight Dodge came to a sliding halt in front of the driveway and he was out of the vehicle with his pistol drawn before the armored SWAT vehicle made it to him. Once the back doors flung open and SWAT officers poured out in pairs, he fell into line with the Alpha group.

At the front door, they awaited radio confirmation that the Bravo team was in place. They could hear from their position on the porch that at least one person was inside moving frantically. Maybe more. The signal came that the Bravo team was in place and as soon as the cackle on the radio ended, Officer Jacobs, the first man in line, kicked the door three times with his heavy boot. He was not trying to kick the door in, but rather give the inhabitants a chance to exit peacefully.

"IMPD," Jack yelled assertively, "We have a warrant! Open the door, or we will!"

Jacobs kicked three more times.

"Last fucking chance!"

When the door remained latched, Jack tapped Officer Jacobs on his right shoulder. Another officer behind him hit the radio, "Going in," and Jacobs did. He hit the latch of the door with a heavy ramrod and the cheap wood splintered as if a breaching charge had been used rather than the steel ram.

Officer Jacobs entered and rolled right as Officer Nixon rolled left. As Jack was about to enter, he heard three shots which caused him to drop to his knees. He stretched his body into the house, leaning to the right, and saw a shirtless man with a bandana over his face shooting an AK-style weapon. Jack let off six shots, each one finding a home in the man's torso.

Nixon called out, "Clear. We need a medic! Jacobs was hit!"

The rest of the team filled in, the last two grabbing Jacobs by the shoulders and pulled him back out of the house.

From the back of the house, Jack heard a flashbang explode, and SWAT ordered more people to get on the ground. Jack went to the man he had exchanged fire with and pulled his bandana from his face. It was not whom he was looking for, so he went down the hall to the left. Half of the SWAT team followed him, the other half checked the various doors and furniture in the living room.

In the hall, Jack found a set of stairs that led up to the second floor. According to their intel, the second floor was where the dealers hung out. There could be as many as five or six up there and they had plenty of guns.

Jack ascended the stairs vigilantly. Each step was more calculated than the one before it and his gun made rhythmic sweeps from left to right. At the top of the steps, Jack realized he could only go one way. Left.

The hall was dark but he could tell there were only two rooms upstairs. They were side-by-side and both doors were closed. He signaled for the team to stop and they did. He listened intently but heard nothing from either room. All he could hear was the sound of officers executing their search downstairs.

Jack signaled for three men to go to the door on the right and two to go with him to the left. Once every man was in position, Jack counted from three to one with his left hand. At one, he kicked in the door, rapidly moving in from left to right. The officer across the door from him did the opposite, and the officer in the middle entered straight ahead.

Jack unexpectedly saw a table standing vertically in the corner. It was clearly out of place and he had worked the job long enough to know criminals were not known for their intelligence. Hence, why they become criminals.

Jack signaled to the table with his hand and the two officers approached it slowly. Jack took the right side, nearest the wall. When in place, he shoved the table to the side and as he expected, someone was hiding behind it.

The man dove at Jack as soon as the light hit him. It was as if he were a wild raccoon that became cornered and decided the best option was to attack. However, it was not. Jack leaned to his left and made a quick spin to his right, moving his left hand up to the shoulder of the man and helping his momentum drive his forehead into the drywall.

There was a thunderous CRACK when the man's head hit causing him to fold to the floor.

Jack knelt beside him and shone his light into the bloody face of the man.

"Fuck, dude!" He said, "This is not legal! You cannot just bust in here and start shooting and shit. I was just defending myself, I thought ya'll be fucking breaking in!"

Jack smacked the man on the side of his head. More with his fingers than his palm, causing a loud snap. It was an attempt to get the man's attention, not to hurt him. "We announced ourselves twice, genius. Now make this easy, Toke. If you don't want to be laced up with your dead partner downstairs, who shot an officer by the way, I suggest you think about chatting with me."

"I'm fucking bleeding everywhere!" Toke, a nineteen-year-old dealer, who Jack had tried to help in the past, was squirming like a child throwing a tantrum. Toke's older brother had been killed in a drive-by six years before. Almost a month later, Toke was arrested for selling crack. Jack was the arresting officer.

"It's just a scratch," Jack told him.

Jack had spent three years trying to get Toke into programs, and rehabs, and even having lunch with him to try and connect. Toke was a smart kid. He had been on the honor roll and part of some national recognition. Jack did not want to see him throw all of that away.

But he had. Now Toke had two felonies and was going to be getting his third. Toke couldn't be saved, and Jack no longer had an interest. He just wanted answers.

"Tell you what, I will get you an ambulance and a night in the hospital if you agree to talk. Otherwise, they'll just stitch you up in the back of the bus and you get to go right to lock up."

'Fine, fuck it. Just get me to a hospital!"

Jack took some extra time writing up his report. He wanted Toke to sweat a little more waiting for the questioning to begin. The first few times Jack would question Toke in connection to a crime, Toke would be nervous. He was like a child knowing he had disappointed his father and getting him to open up was easy because he trusted and respected Jack. Now, Toke was deep in the life and Jack was just another cop. Or he was the father who had been disappointed enough times that the child no longer cared to do better.

Two hours after Toke had been admitted, scanned, and bandaged up he was put into a private room on the top floor. Two officers stood guard in plain sight so Toke knew he could not escape. He had also been cuffed to the plastic rails of the bed and his door locked. Jack knew he would be using the time to come up with a lie. Either a lie about why he was in the trap house or a lie about the twenty pounds of drugs they found and the dozens of illegal weapons. But those were not at the top of Jack's concerns.

Jack wanted to know what the drug was and who the supplier was. The lab had made a preliminary confirmation that the drugs found were the same in Cheddar's system, and they had never seen it before. It appeared to be a cross between heroin and cocaine. But it was not the typical speedball they would find; it was more potent and there were other traces of drugs and plants they had not yet identified.

It took Jack twenty minutes to walk from the precinct to the hospital, another ten to get to the top floor, and another five to talk to the officer on guard. In total, Toke had spent almost four hours awaiting the questioning process. Jack knew that Toke had been grilled enough over the past couple of years that he had developed somewhat of a knack for not answering questions. While some criminals blabbed others lawyered up, Toke just said nothing.

Jack entered the dim room and for a moment, he could still see the scared kid in Toke's face. When he saw Jack standing at the door he scuffed and turned his eyes to fix on an arbitrary point on the far wall. His eyes were glued there.

"I got nothin' to say, man."

Jack walked over to the bed blinking his eyes rapidly to wash the sight of the child from his sight and replace it with the criminal before him. He pulled a metal chair from its place against the wall and sat down only a foot from Toke.

"Why were you in that trap house?"

Toke's eyes stayed glued on the invisible point and he clenched his teeth.

Laying there, Jack thought, Toke looked like more than just a child. He looked broken. A thick bandage wrapped around his head and his left eye had begun to darken with a bruise. On a normal day, Toke looked like any other nineteen-year-old, but his eyes held a darkness that said he was just a little bit different from the rest. Now, in that bed, he was but a remnant of that character.

"I guess you know Cheddar OD'd?"

Silence.

"The drugs in his system are the same drugs we found in that stash house today, which is pretty bad news for you, bub."

Toke's eyes remained glued on the imaginary point, but he spoke. "Why is that?"

"See, the drugs in his system are rare. We haven't seen anything like it before. This means it won't be hard to convince a jury that you are the one who sold it to him."

"Yeah, well…"

Jack felt his chest tighten and his throat constricted in unison. He normally did not care if a perp were willing to throw their life away for "the code of the street." But he could not shake the site of the thirteen-year-old kid he remembered and it pissed him off. It was a bullshit code that had cost a lot of people a lot of time and a lot of pain.

"Dammit, Jamal!"

At this, Toke took his eyes off his target and looked at Jack a little startled. No one had called him by his real name in years, and certainly not with such a tone of disappointment.

"You want to throw away your life for some guys who are going to flip on you the second I step into an interrogation? What the fuck happened, man? You know you could have come to me at any time, and I would have helped you. Why go down this road and waste all the talents you have?"

"Help me?" Toke's words weighed with an offense. "In case you forgot, Detective, I did come to you. Two years ago. Remember?"

Jack just looked at him.

"I told you some dudes on my block had it out for me and they were going to hurt me. You told me, 'walk away like a man.'" Toke rolled his eyes, "But my crew was there for me, and they made sure I was okay when the time came."

Jack leaned closer to Toke. "I'm sorry I let you down, Jamal." He let out a deep breath, "When I would go to my old man, he would tell me, 'A man takes care of his own business and takes what comes with it.' That's all I knew. I did not know that, that wasn't what you needed from me."

"Well, too late now, ain't it?"

Jack lowered his voice to a near whisper. "No. Only if you give up. Then it's too late. I think you still have all the ability in the world to be whatever you want to be, man. You are smart and young, and you are better than this. But for real, this *is* your last chance. If I walk out of this room, I cannot help you. When I walk out of here and I go talk to your buddies and they flip on you, you are going to prison, and all that goes to waste."

Jack saw a tear in the corner of Toke's eye but he said nothing. He returned his gaze to the imaginary spot on the wall and swallowed hard.

"Okay, then…" Jack stood from the chair and turned towards the door. He began walking slowly, a part of him hoping Jamal would ask him to stay. To tell Jack everything and with that, give him a chance to start over. When he reached the door, all hope faded when his hand wrapped the handle.

"Wait…"

Jack stopped and turned to face Jamal.

"The shit is called Blood Thorn. One of the active ingredients to the root of the blood-thorn rose and it feels like your blood is boiling. The high is supposed to be super intense and the fiends can't get enough of it."

"Tell me everything, Jamal." He stepped back towards the chair. "Everything."

CHAPTER 28

Deputy Carl took the Neils into their home to get their statements while Sheriff Tom stood on the beach with David.

"So, tell me what you saw," Sheriff Tom said as he pulled a flip notepad from his breast pocket.

"I didn't see much," David told him. "I was at my rental when I heard Mrs. Ogletree screaming. I came running down the beach and found Dr. Neil comforting her. I checked the roses and saw the body."

"And you say you know Braden?"

"Can I be honest with you, Sheriff?"

Sheriff Tom's face showed a sign of intrigue. He put the pen and pad to his side and tilted his head back as if he were about to close the case in record time. "I would prefer it."

"I am a therapist from Indianapolis. Braden and his wife were my clients… Though over the past few months more so Caroline than Braden. He stopped attending sessions."

"Uh-huh?"

"Caroline had mentioned that she was going to file for divorce and she was scared. Not of Braden, I don't think. More just the change and all that comes with divorce. But she missed her next session and no one could get in contact with her. The IMPD wasn't moving as fast as I would have liked."

"So, you thought it would be a good idea to come up here and look around yourself?"

David shrugged. "I just wanted to see if they were here. My only concern was their safety. If I got here and found out they were safe I would have left and let them reach out on their own time. But of course, I never did find them and so I was sticking around to see if I could figure out where they might be."

"Well, you found one of them," Sheriff Tom said pointing to the rose bushes.

"I know this must look pretty bad."

"Doesn't look great, I have to be honest."

"My buddy Jack is a detective for IMPD, he can verify everything."

"We do not get any crime up here, as I have told you. I may be a little rusty when it comes to murder and violent crime, but you do not strike me as a cold-blooded killer. I believe what you're telling me, but you're going to have to stick around until we get this thing figured out."

"I understand." The two men turned their attention to the body as three men with a gurney began their descent towards them from Dr. Neil's home.

"How do you think he was murdered?"

"Won't know until we get the ME report, but looks like some bruising around the neck and blood on his scalp. Could be strangulation or blunt force, but really cannot be positive. Could have been shot for all I know. It is strange to leave them in the blood-thorns though."

"The what?"

"Blood-thorn roses. Mr. Roads saw them somewhere and liked them, so in the development of the community he slated this spot to be a patch."

"Think someone was trying to send him a message?"

Sheriff Tom shrugged. "Whomever it was wanted the body found. So, seems like they were sending a message to someone. Just do not know who."

"I would like to help you with this case, Sheriff."

Sheriff Tom chuckled, "I appreciate that, David. I do. But I cannot let a civilian—an out-of-towner at that—get involved."

"I will not get in the way, Sheriff. I want to find out who did this just as much as you and you do not have much of a force here, remember. I assume this is staying close to the vest?"

"We won't be bringing in city or state if that's what you mean?"

187

"I am a therapist. I can help you get inside the killer's mind, like the forensic psychiatrists the big guys have."

David could tell Sheriff Tom had not considered this. But somehow, the sheriff did not know that himself, "That is exactly what I was thinking. Meet me at the station tomorrow morning. We should have the ME report by then and know a little more. In the meantime, I will put out an APB on Caroline and schedule a town hall."

"Won't all of that bring in bigger departments?"

"No," he said, "Our ME is the resident doctor at the clinic on the other side of Havana. She has her own people run the tests so other departments don't catch wind. And the APB will be broad."

David did not say anything else, but it sounded to him like a criminal enterprise running a police investigation more than an up-and-up police agency. He guessed Sheriff Tom could sense his concerns because he addressed them.

"It is standard operating procedure for private police and security. Which we are. We are not city or state funded."

CHAPTER 29

David spent the next few hours with thoughts racing. Who would want Braden dead? Why would they want him dead? David did not know him too well, outside of their few sessions and what Caroline had told him, but he seemed like a decent man. He could lash out when stressed, but even then, he seemed to reserve himself. He did not seem like the type of man who would stack up a list of deadly enemies.

David's thoughts returned to the ledger. The answer, he knew, was probably in there. Or, that was the answer. Whatever it was that Braden had been keeping track of was enough to get him killed. To David, it was nothing but pages of numbers and initials, but to someone, it was much more.

As the sun set behind the lake, David's thoughts were torn from the murder of Braden to his phone, which blasted the silence with a repeated ringing. It was Jack.

"Hey, how was the bust?"

"Good. I got what I needed."

"Well, that is good. Listen, there was a body that was discovered here tonight."

Silence fell over the line. Then, Jack spoke, "In Havana?"

"Yes. It was Braden. Someone wanted to make a message about it, too."

"I bet it has to do with the ledger."

David nodded in agreement as if Jack could see him. Even though he could not, the two had been friends long enough that they seemed to have telepathic abilities when it came to what the other was thinking.

"You were thinking the same thing, weren't you?"

"I was."

"I think I may have something that will help. Actually, I will be heading that way tomorrow."

"Really? What? Why?"

"The kid I busted said that the drugs coming in are coming from up there. He thought Chicago but had heard the term 'Havana' by some of his fellow goons. He thought it was a crew from Chicago, now, I think they are the ones pumping drugs into the city."

"And Braden had something to do with it?"

"Or he knew who did."

"You ever hear of someone dumping a body in a patch of flowers? Like trying to hide it long enough for evidence to be taken away, but not so that it would never be found?"

Jack thought for a moment, "No, usually the goal is to make sure the body is never found. It is infinitely harder to charge and convict someone for murder if there is no body. And the street gangs will just leave them where they drop."

"Well, someone dumped him in a patch of blood-thorn roses."

The line fell silent again, but this time David noticed it was different. Whatever caused Jack to go silent was something important.

"Jack," David finally said when he thought the call may have dropped.

"Where did you say he was found?"

"In a patch of blood-thorn roses."

"No shit?"

David could almost hear Jack's brain turning on the other end of the line. "Guess what the name of the drug flooding our streets is called."

"Blood Thorn?"

"Yes. One of the main fucking ingredients."

"So, we know the where. Maybe the why. We just need to figure out the who."

"Listen, fuck tomorrow. I am coming to town tonight and I am going to have to keep a low profile. I don't want the whole town to know a city cop is out there. So, you are gonna have to help me out, pal."

"Well lucky for you, I am riding shotgun with the sheriff tomorrow to work this thing. Is your captain going to be okay with you doing this?"

Jack laughed a deep roaring laugh which caused David to pull the phone from his ear. "Fucking Andy Griffith out to solve the drug case of the year! Perfect! The captain will be fine with it. I will just tell him I need a few days to follow up on a lead up north. You let me handle that."

"Perfect. I will be able to get you information." David looked over at the clock on the stove. It was 10 p.m. "You really plan on coming tonight? It will be almost one in the morning before you get here."

"Good, everyone will be asleep. I just have to figure out how to get in the gates without drawing any attention."

David smirked as an idea crossed his mind, "I think I can take care of that, as well."

David hung up with Bella and quickly sent a text to Jack. Jack was to meet Bella at her apartment at five the next morning. She would slip him into the trunk of her roommate's car and bring him to David's.

Most of the community knew Bella and David were getting closer, he was sure Dr. Neil was not the only one. A community operating as Havana did would not have many secrets. Other than the kind that got people killed. Bella would back up to the garage which was out of view of any neighbor. Jack would emerge from the trunk and no one would have a clue. Two hours later, David would be at the sheriff's office to meet Sheriff Tom.

Then David called his mother to let her know he would be in town for a few more days than expected. He needed her to inform all his clients as well as send them referrals for other therapists if they needed them. He had built a strong rapport with most of his clients and he doubted that any of them would be willing to go to a new therapist. He could not give a definite date of return, but he hoped that it would be soon. He needed answers.

David set his alarm to be up at 5 a.m., double-checked the windows and doors, then went upstairs to catch a few hours of sleep.

CHAPTER 30

At 5:30 a.m. Bella's car backed into the driveway, she maneuvered the back half of the car into the garage, shielding it from the view of the rest of the world. The trunk clicked and Jack burst from the dwelling nearly knocking David to the ground in the process.

"Damnit I am glad to be out of there!" Jack's voice was gravelly and his words came out rapidly.

Bella stepped out of the car and approached David and Jack, taking a spot next to David. "First time I have ever smuggled someone in the trunk of a car. Glad it was a cop though, at least I know I will not be spending the best years of my life behind bars."

David smiled and put an arm around her. "Thank you for doing this. I know you didn't have to."

"I guess I needed a little more excitement in my life," she turned to David. "Come see me after you finish up with Tom?"

"You can count on it."

Bella stood on the tips of her toes and kissed David. She then turned to Jack, "It was nice to meet you. Hopefully next time I won't be trying to fit you into a trunk."

Jack's eyes were wide as he shut the trunk for Bella but they remained on David as she got into the car and drove off.

"You know, there are quite a few details you didn't mention in our last conversation."

"What do you mean?"

"You are in town a few days and already pulling the hottest chick you have ever dated? What the hell man?"

David felt his cheeks warm, "It kind of just happened."

"You know, I have never pulled a babe when I was investigating something. How'd you do it?"

"Man, I got to meet the sheriff. You want some sleep?"

"Yes, actually. That sounds like the best idea I have ever heard."

"Okay, there is a guest room upstairs—it is the one without my stuff—you can crash in there. There's a little bit of food but not much. I will bring some dinner back from the diner."

"This place has a diner too?"

David nodded, "It is pretty much its own small town. A store, a diner, things like that."

"I'll be damned."

"I don't know how long Sheriff Tom will want to keep me around, but make yourself at home."

"I guess as long as it takes to make sure you aren't going to blab about the body in paradise. Or long enough to make sure that you aren't the one who put a bullet in the man."

"Sheriff Tom thinks it was blunt force trauma."

Jack rolled his eyes and scoffed, "It is a figure of speech, smart guy."

A half-hour later David made his way into the Sheriff's Department with a box of muffins Bella had set aside for him. He knew that some—if not all—of the deputies would be wary of him tagging along during the investigation. He knew that food was a universal symbol of peace, and he needed as many of them on his side as possible. Especially, as Jack pointed out, crooked cops are everywhere. But in a place like Havana, they had more to gain from being dirty than a regular street cop in the city.

David was greeted by an elderly woman who sat behind a desk that appeared to have almost been a second—maybe even a third—thought after the building had been opened. As if the decorators remembered at the last second someone would need to greet visitors and the desk that sat there was the only thing they could find on short notice. It was agonizingly out of place with the rest of the town and even with the building, which had wooden floors and shiplap walls, giving it a modern and sleek look.

A sixty-five-inch television hung from the wall behind the elderly woman, showcasing the weather in Havana and the water conditions. On the bottom was a rolling scroll of police bulletins from the surrounding cities, including Chicago, which had the most screen time.

"Hello, sir. How can I direct you?" The woman's voice was shaky. She was about his mother's age but seemed to lack the life and luster. She looked as though she could be Sheriff Tom's older sister, but acted as though she could be his mother.

"I am here to meet the sheriff," David told her.

"Oh, you must be David. Tom said you would be coming in today." The woman stood from the plastic chair behind the grotesque desk with more vibrance than her body seemed capable of. She led him through a set of double doors to her right and down a long bright corridor also decorated in sleek wood flooring and shiplap walls. Framed pictures of deputies lined the walls.

"How many officers are on duty here?" David asked, amazed at the number of faces on the wall. He was unsure of why a town this small and free of crime would need such a heavy police presence.

The woman stopped and let her mind calculate. "Oh, besides Tom, I would say four deputies and maybe two volunteers."

That was more what he had expected. "Who are all of these officers on the walls?"

The woman turned to David and smiled. "These are officers who have given their lives over the past decade in the surrounding counties. Some are family of the officers here, but most are fallen heroes. The boys put them up to remind them of the sacrifice some officers must make."

The woman led him further down the corridor to another set of double doors. Once inside he saw four deputies, including Deputy Carl, sitting at desks scattered in no particular arrangement and eying him suspiciously. He guessed more than some of them thumbed him as the killer. The outsider who wandered into their little paradise, and now someone was dead.

The woman stopped in the middle of the room, seemingly unfazed by the laser eyes staring them down. She pointed to a closed door with blinds on the other side of the glass drawn. On the door in white stencil was the word 'Sheriff.' "Tom is in there. Just give a little knock and he will call you in."

"Thank you, Ma'am."

"Oh," the woman said, "Ma'am is what you'd call my mother." David assumed her mother would have been deceased for at least a decade. Unless her mother started childbearing in middle school. "I am Janet. Anything you need, just let me know."

"Thank you, Janet."

David kept the hot eyes of the deputies to his back. He did not want to make eye contact with any of them, not until the sheriff gave him a stamp of approval. David knew they would not trust him otherwise, and if he tried to be friendly, they would only become more suspicious. Instead, he put the box of muffins on a table beside him, then he gave two gentle knocks on the door. As soon as his hand left the door on the second knock, Sheriff Tom called him in.

"Mr. Thorne. I was not expecting you so early."

"I am nothing if not prompt."

The sheriff pointed to a wingback chair on the opposite side of his desk where he sat. Unlike Janet's desk—and workstation in general—thought had gone into the sheriff's arrangement. The walls were a pristine pearl, the hardwood flooring smelled of fresh Pine-Sol. His desk was a deep brown which looked like Maple, the grain of the wood accentuated. He had a new-looking desktop computer, a file cabinet behind his right shoulder, and a neat stack of files on his desk. David sat in the leather chair.

"This stack of files here is everything I have on Braden Baker. The COD from the ME, his business records, and his criminal record."

"Seems like quite the stack. Was he familiar with a life of crime?"

"Actually," the sheriff said splitting the stack in half. "He had one arrest when he was nineteen for a DUI. Outside of that, he was clean. One of these files is from the ME."

"And the rest?"

"All business files. Companies he owned, companies he worked for, and financial files. All the things we think might get a man killed."

David nodded, impressed, "So, you suspect someone killed him over money?"

"In my experience, Mr. Thorne, a man finds himself dead for one of two reasons. Money or a woman."

David nodded, showing his agreement, "And you believe Braden was killed over the former."

"The examiner put in her report that he had two small caliber bullet holes in the back of his head. He had, at some point before his death, been punched at least twice in the face and bound by duct tape."

"Seems pretty rough just for money or business dispute."

"Not really. If it were a crime of passion, such as being over a woman, the beating would have been worse and he would have been shot with a full magazine. Whoever did this was sending a point and did just enough to make sure the job was done. In fact," the sheriff leaned back in his chair and paused as if contemplating how he wanted to continue. "It feels professional to me."

"Like a hit?" This caught David's attention. Who would put a professional hit out on Braden? What could he have been into that would require such viciousness?

"Exactly."

There was a knock at the door and the sheriff summoned the visitor. It was Deputy Carl. He entered the office and closed the door behind him.

"What is it, Deputy?"

"With all due respect, sir, do you really think it is a good idea to share sensitive information with this guy? We are more than capable of handling this in-house." Deputy Carl looked at David as he spoke, making his stance crystal clear.

"Thank you for your concern, Deputy. And I know you and the boys are more than capable. But if we want to keep this confined to the community, we need all the help we can get. Is that all?"

"Yes, sir."

"Then why don't you take one of the guys back to the scene and see if you can find anything that might help us? And send the rest of the crew to the Baker residence."

"Yes, sir." Deputy carl gave David one last look of warning, then left.

"He isn't much of a fan of outsiders, huh?"

"He is a good kid. He grew up outside the gates, so he takes his job seriously. It isn't personal… it's just personal."

Somehow, that had made sense to David. "So, what do we do?"

A grim look came over the sheriff's face, "Caroline is considered a missing person. Whoever did this, probably has her. If he hasn't killed her already. Or she had something to do with it."

A cold rush of pain shot through David's stomach. He had considered that fact the night before but was able to push it aside. Now, with the words floating in the air, the realness of the possibility pained him.

"If she is dead," the sheriff continued, "we need to find the body. If she isn't, then may God help us find her."

"Where do we go first?"

"I know a place. Let's roll."

CHAPTER 31

The "place" to which the sheriff had been referring was a dilapidated building that mirrored a collapsed barn butted to the edge of a wooded area on the west end of the community. They had driven the sheriff's jeep out to the beach and continued two miles past David's rental. When they arrived at the remains of the beaten building David followed Sheriff Tom out to the beach.

"I am surprised to see something like this out here."

The sheriff nodded in agreement, "It used to be some sort of fishing shack years ago. This whole area is the last of the construction, which will eventually be a banquette hall. But when the tide is out some of the folks from outside can get across and they use the area for fooling around. We typically sweep the area every night, but haven't had to in a while."

The sheriff walked towards the pile of boards and destroyed roof and began kicking pieces with his foot. David could not tell if he was kicking for the sake of it, or if he was looking for something.

"You think that has something to do with what happened to Braden? Attacked by someone who snuck in? Why not leave his body here if he was attacked here?"

"Don't look for rationale in violence, son. It is a waste of time."

David knew that to be true. He began sifting through the decay with his foot. He decided he would look for anything that looked like a weapon or blood. If he were supposed to be looking for anything else, he knew he would never notice it.

"Got something," the sheriff said. His voice was low and lacked any excitement David might have expected.

David walked over to the sheriff as he held up a piece of gray plastic. "Braden's driver's license."

David looked at the sand and soot-covered card in the sheriff's hand. It was his ID, but it did not make sense. Why attack Braden clear on the other side of the beach and drag him past several houses just to dump him in the roses? There was more than enough garbage here to conceal the body. Not to mention the risk someone would be taking just to move it. Unless, David thought…

"What if someone planted that there?"

The sheriff gave him a quizzical glare, "Why in the world would they do that?"

"To throw you off," David said bluntly. "They put the body somewhere it was sure to be found. They wanted that. But maybe they didn't want you to know where he was attacked."

David could see the sheriff's mind following the trail. "If they put that here, you assume he was attacked here. But that does not add up, does it? To kill him here and then move his body two miles and past several houses?"

"Can't say that it does." The sheriff pondered the new theory. "But why not just leave the ID on Braden? And how would they know we would even search here?"

David thought for a moment, "Well, it was the first place you thought of. Maybe it's someone that knows what you would do."

"No one in Havana would do something like this. These are good people, David."

"I am sure they are. But what person from outside would go through all that effort? Wouldn't they just shoot him and leave him where he fell?"

"That is a good point."

"And then to take his wife. This was personal."

"Personal enough that maybe she was in on it." The sheriff tucked the ID into his pocket. David felt a coldness hit his stomach that radiated out. He could not buy that Caroline would be in on her husband's murder. Even as unhappy as she may have been in the marriage, she was a long way off from murder. Besides, this was not as much about passion as proving a point.

"It feels personal, for sure," David conceded. "But not that personal. It was not like he was stabbed a dozen times. He was not shot in the heart or poisoned. Those are what women do in crimes of passion, not shoot them twice in the back of the head, and then hide them in a bed of roses."

"Let's see what the boys found at the house and see if anything goes with this puzzle."

꙳

His eyes opened slowly but some kind of liquid blurred his vision and his pounding head let out echoes between his ears. The pain radiated the entire circumference of his skull, it was a pain that he had never experienced. He vaguely remembered walking down the shore near the loading docks, ready for the next shipment to radio in. Then he heard a crack and everything went dark.

His eyes finally began to sharpen but the liquid prevented him from seeing as clearly as he would have liked. He could not tell if the soft bobbing and floating he felt was from being on the water or from the pain in his head, but he did not like either option. Finally, he was able to make out the shape of two figures. A few moments later, as his eyes cleared more and his vision returned, he identified them.

To his left, the figure towered tall and cloaked in black like the grim reaper coming to collect. To his right stood the boss. He noticed, only then, that his hands were tied by a rope behind his back and his body anchored to a flimsy wooden chair. He thought if he fell back, it would break and he could make a run for it. But the constant motion he felt nearly made him sick, and he could hardly find the strength to raise his head.

"Chanceler," the boss said, his voice low. It almost sounded like a bark. It reminded him of a judge he knew years ago. "You thought I wouldn't notice?"

His voice echoed in his ears, bouncing between the thuds and the loud whistle coming from the ache on the back of his skull. It took him a moment to process what he had been asked. "Notice what?" It hurt to talk, but he knew the consequences of silence.

"Don't fucking play dumb with me. I am missing almost half a million dollars and you are the only other one who has access to the books."

Chanceler shook his head, "I don't ever touch the money, boss. I am not stupid."

The boss laughed and it bellowed. He was not afraid of being heard, which told Chanceler the rocking he felt was probably from being on the water. His insides went cold.

"You may not be stupid, but you are a cocky son-of-a-bitch. You probably didn't think I would notice. Or that you could smooth-talk your way out of it. Aren't those what lawyers are good at?" He looked over to the figure that now stood behind him. It nodded.

"I would not try and cross you. I swear." Now Chanceler was sure he was going to vomit. Between the rocking, the pounding of his skull, and the fear coursing through his veins, he was not sure how long he could hold it.

"Then tell me who else it could have been. If it wasn't you, you must have an idea of who else would have been able to move that kind of money?"

"Smith did the books two months ago. Maybe it was him! I swear to God it wasn't me!"

The boss could see the terror in Chanceler's eyes and it made his lips curl in a ghoulish way. The figure behind him became excited at the onset of the fear as if he could smell it. Like a bell signifying it was time to eat and Chanceler was the prey.

"Yeah, I checked on that. Turns out you looked over the books the following week, remember? To ensure no errors."

"I swear I didn't touch your fucking money!" His voice came out shaky with tears on the edge of every word. His mouth felt dry and each syllable was like sandpaper scraping the roof of his mouth.

"I wish I believed you…"

Chanceler saw the figure draw a large blade from his hip. The moon reflected against the pristinely polished steel. Chanceler's guts vacated when the figure took a step towards him, pushing the razor edge of the blade to the top of his right shoulder.

CHAPTER 32

David returned to his rental just after 9 p.m. and his brain was hot, more questions than answers remained. Sheriff Tom had left at 7 p.m. to speak with the ME and asked David to work with a deputy reading through Braden's files.

David entered the house from the front door and when he rounded the corner leading to the kitchen, he found Jack and Bella sitting at the island drinking beer and laughing.

"This can't be good," David said grabbing his own beer from the iced bucket in the center of the island. The bottle of Miller was icy to the touch.

"Jack was just telling me some stories about you."

David nodded his head, "Well they are probably based in truth but generally exaggerated."

"Did you really pee on a cop from a balcony in grad school?"

David felt the blood rush to his face. The one major party he had attended in college was held by the largest frat on campus. During his undergrad, he had been so focused on courses that he did not take the time to go out much. Jack came to visit him during his first semester in grad school and naturally forced him to take a break from his studies. They managed to get into some party being thrown in an apartment complex. Presumably, so the frat would not catch the brunt of any issues that came down. David caught up with his five years' worth of college partying in the first two hours. Which was about when all the alcohol decided it needed to escape his body, as well. He stumbled to the balcony—which he swore was the bathroom—and started to go. He heard screaming that was muffled and far away, then he saw Jack laughing and pulling him by the arm, a trail of urine following him. Jack rushed him down a back staircase, mostly carrying David, and out into an alley.

David recalled the story to Bella. She fell into hysterics.

"He said you left a trail through the entire apartment."

David shrugged, "That would explain why no one talked to me for a few months after."

"David is a serious worker. All work and no play…"

"Make me a dull boy, I know."

"I don't know," Bella chimed in. "He has been pretty fun so far." She leaned her body into him and he wrapped an arm around her shoulder.

"Speaking of work," Jack said, "anything?"

"Sorta, but not really. There is an old collapsed building at the far end of the beach where people might go to party. It is pretty secluded. Some of Braden's belongings were found there. The sheriff thinks he stumbled across something he shouldn't have and they killed him. Or that Caroline was in on it somehow. They did not find anything at his house, which I already knew."

"Better hope they don't find a certain set of prints," Jack told him.

"They won't." He took a long swig from his bottle. "What about you? Were you able to do anything useful while you were here? Besides, tell my lovely lady friend embarrassing stories about me."

Jack smirked, "Actually, yes. I told one of my buddies in Chicago to keep an eye out for suspicious ships like you described. He hadn't seen anything but a body washed up on a beach about thirty minutes ago." He turned to Bella, "right?"

She confirmed with a nod.

"What is so special about that?"

Jack leaned back with a smug look on his face. "He was an attorney. Chanceler Wells."

David thought hard, "Why does that name sound so familiar?"

"Because he has a house here," Bella told him. "He would have been at that party Dr. Neil threw. You probably saw him there." Bella's face softened, "So sad. He had a wife and two girls. I think he even had a grandson on the way."

"That is interesting," David said. "What did he say about the body?"

"Mutilated. Someone worked hard to hide his identity. They even tied something to his feet to keep him at the bottom of the lake. Somehow it was severed and he floated ashore. Whoever put him there probably wasn't counting on him ever being found."

"Then why try to hide his identity?" Bella asked.

"Just in case. Whoever is behind these murders is not a first-timer," David pointed out. "They are doing an awful lot to try and throw the police off."

"What doesn't make sense," Jack said. "Is that Braden was kept here, in Havana. Chanceler was dropped in the lake. A body found here, as we know, is kept quiet and no outsiders are privy to it. No one in Chicago or Indy has received word of Braden's murder."

"Makes sense though, if one body winds up here it is scary. But two would send all these mega-wealthy homeowners running. Havana can't have that. If Chanceler is found somewhere else—anywhere else—it can be pushed off as being in the wrong place at the wrong time."

"Two men from Havana wind up dead within a week of one another. That is not a coincidence." Jack said popping the top off a new bottle.

"There is no such thing as coincidence," David reminded him. "But if there were, I would agree with you. This isn't one of them."

"Why would anyone want to kill people from Havana? Jealousy?" Bella was struggling to understand how the peaceful and serine place she had become a part of could have a violent underbelly. It seemed unfathomable to her. Outside of those gates, it was nothing new. Murder and mayhem were part of life, but inside, it was supposed to be different.

"We need to figure out what they had in common. What did these two men do or know that would get them killed."

"How do you want to go about it?"

David thought for a moment, "I am going to the ME with Sheriff Tom tomorrow and then we are reviewing some of his belongings. I will hopefully have some answers then. I want you to dig into Chanecler's life. Find out anything and everything and maybe there will be something there."

"How can I help?" Bella asked.

"I don't want you involved," David told her honestly. "There is someone out there killing people from Havana. Either because of something they did or something they know. I won't put you in danger by bringing you into this."

"I promise to do what you and Jack say. I won't ask anyone anything you two don't say I should." She leaned toward David and put her right hand on his cheek. "Besides you don't grow up in The Region without learning how to defend yourself."

Jack tilted his bottle in her direction. "Woman has a point."

After Jack had retired to bed David grabbed two wine glasses and a bottle of Cabernet Sauvignon then he and Bella made their way out onto the deck and down to the beach. Bella laid out a plaid blanket in the soft sand and the two sat under the stars. David poured each of them a glass. David took a sip. It was dry and full-bodied but had a pleasant fruitiness to it.

Bella watched the water's stillness, which looked almost like glass in the calm night. The moon high above them reflected off the mirror surface and cast a white hue across miles of the glassed water.

"This is so beautiful," she said, "I could only dream of living in a place like this."

"Indianapolis doesn't have anything like this, but it has its beauty and eloquence."

"I went with my parents to see the Children's Museum once. I think we went to the zoo also. But usually, we always went to Chicago."

"You should come down sometime and I will show you around. Your personal tour guide."

Bella smiled and leaned into him. "Do you think we would work? I mean in the real world?"

David pulled her closer to him. "What do you mean? This is the real world, right now."

"I mean you being a famous therapist living with the high rollers. Then me, a girl from here with a waitress job working for the high rollers."

David knew what she meant, "My clients are rich, yes, but most are not famous. And I spend more time with Jack and my mother than I do with any high rollers. My life is not that complicated, Bella. I am not a particularly vain man. Where you grew up and what you do for work is not my concern. Being with you is. Seeing you smile is. Holding you right now is what I care about. Not whether someone else thinks we fit into their perception of the world and how it should work."

Bella looked up at him, the high moon reflected a soft hue of white from her skin giving her the appearance of an angel, David thought. He leaned in a kissed her deeply. She allowed her body to fall back onto the blanket, the glasses crashed to the sand as their bodies began to join and it became impossible to tell where one began and the other ended.

Bella pulled at the buttons on David's shirt, slowly revealing the flesh on his chest, and then his back as she peeled it from his body.

"I want you," she whispered into his ear before playfully biting at the lobe.

So, David gave himself to her. All of himself.

CHAPTER 33

The next morning David rolled himself out from under Bella and hopped into the shower. Even though he had showered the night before with Bella, he still felt granules of sand falling from his scalp. A bit of him felt guilty. He had not been with a woman—at least not so completely—since Alice. It had been almost fifteen years. He knew that the guilt was unjust.

Once he finished the shower he dressed, kissed Bella on her forehead, and lightly made his way down the steps. Jack slid him a cup of coffee as he took a zealous bite from his bagel.

"My man! I might have to rent my own place here if you two are going to be making that kind of racket all night."

David shot him a glare. "A little decorum, Jack. Bella is not a one-night thing."

Jack threw his hand up and spoke with a chunk of bagel in his cheek. "I am glad to hear it. God knows it has been long enough."

"Are you making yourself useful today?"

"While you are with Sheriff Fife, I will be running a background on the dead lawyer and see if anything blends with Braden."

"Barney Fife was the deputy. Andy Taylor was the sheriff." David grabbed the last half of the bagel and headed for the front door.

From behind his shoulder, he heard Jack yell, "I am glad you got a woman. You have been spending too much time with your mom."

David met Sheriff Tom just outside the station. The sheriff had a grim look on his face, David suspected it had to do with Chanceler's body being found.

"What's going on?"

"Another body was found."

"Here? In Havana?"

The sheriff let out a heavy sigh, "No, thank God. It was found on a beach in Chicago. But it was a resident here."

"Do they suspect foul play?"

"Yes, it was brutal. Tried to weigh the body down in the lake but the ropes must have been cut by rocks."

David grimaced, even knowing the information already did not make it any easier to stomach. "So, someone is killing off Havana residents. Still think Caroline might have had something to do with this?"

The sheriff shook his head. "It is looking less and less likely." Sheriff Tom began walking towards

219

his vehicle. "We have to go talk with the widow. Do you have any experience in grief counseling?"

"Some."

"Good," he said, his voice low and saddened. "It will come in handy."

The drive to the house took only ten minutes. The house was nestled deep in a set of woods and up a hill, uniquely different from most of the houses on the compound which rested on the shore.

"Do you and the deputies have property in Havana," David asked.

"Not exactly. Some of the deputies who are volunteers do. But the four employed deputies stay in a dorm behind the precinct. They get all the perks of living in Havana without the cost. Free apartment, free food, and free gas. It isn't bad."

"And you?"

"I have a ranch in the center of Havana. A perk of being Sheriff."

"Deputy Ringwall stay in the dorm, too?"

"Yeah, poor fella has no life. Straight from work to his room. Rinse and repeat."

David nodded as if he understood. "It is hard to be young and single."

"I can only imagine."

"How is the pay," David asked changing the subject before Sheriff Tom could question David about his curiosities.

"Better than the outside," he said. "We are called a Sheriff's Department, but in all truth, we are more like private security. But I assure you, we are every bit as professional as outside law enforcement. Many of us have a history in the military or law enforcement."

Once through the woods, the house came into view and David psychically felt his jaw drop. The three-story house sat on the hill like an ancient castle. The home was made of dark gray stone with two watch towers on either side, completing the castle façade. There was a gap in the trees behind the home, allowing for a perfect view of the lake behind it.

The front door looked to be the better part of nine feet in height and to be made of sturdy wood.

Sheriff Tom parked in front of the house and the two made their way across a bridge that hovered over a mini-moat. Something David had not noticed until he was right over it.

"They like the castle look, huh?"

"Chanceler was supposedly ninety-percent Scottish and this was his acknowledgment of that heritage."

Sheriff Tom knocked on the door. Only seconds later a woman David vaguely recognized from Dr. Neil's party answered the door. Her dark brunette hair had been tied in a bun pulling her slightly aged face taught. Her makeup had been applied with artistic precision. She wore a navy dress that hugged her frame and complemented it well.

"Sheriff Tom," she said, but David thought the surprise in her voice was less sincere than she wanted it to be. Tom did not seem to notice.

"Mary, may we come in?"

Mary gave David a look that seemed to say, "Who is this man I have never met?"

"This is David Thorne," Tom told her. "He is working with the Sheriff's department for a time."

"Of course," she slid her body only slightly using her right hand to point them into the house. Sheriff Tom and David were forced to brush against her to enter and David thought she had done that intentionally.

The interior of the home did not match the exterior. Unlike the old castle feel of the outside, the inside was decorated post-modern. Artwork lined much of the wall space, leaving little of the paint beneath it visible. The floor was wood and the furniture was white leather. Even the light fixtures along the wall and the chandelier that hung from the ceiling were modern. But it was the view that caught David by surprise. The back wall was floor-to-ceiling glass and stretched the entire length of the room, and it looked out to the lake beyond. Their beach space was at least three times the size of David's.

"Your home is beautiful," David told her.

"It is." She turned her attention to the sheriff. "Can I get you, boys, anything? Water or tea? I have some coffee in the pot, I just made it."

"No thank you," Sheriff Tom said with a slight bow. "Can we sit?"

"Absolutely."

The three of them sat. Tom and David sat side by side on the white sofa while Mary took a chair beside the fireplace. "I am afraid I have some bad news."

"What is it?" Mary's face grew concerned and her arms crossed over her body. A sign, David knew, of self-protection.

"Chanceler was found dead last night. In Chicago. Do you know where he was last night?"

"Dead?" Her voice began to shake. Tears formed in the corners of her eyes and without hesitation, she blocked them from ruining her fresh makeup. "How? What happened?"

Sheriff Tom looked for an easy way to say the words. A way to tell the widow without sharing the horrific details. Then, he decided, there was not an easy way. "It appears he was murdered."

"Oh my, God!"

"Do you know why he would have been in Chicago? Did he say anything to you last night?"

Mary thought for a moment, "No. He said he had to meet with someone at about six. But he did not say who or where."

"Was it odd that he was not here when you woke up this morning," David asked softly, leaning in closer to her to help her feel connected.

"Not really. He would regularly go fishing or golfing and be gone before I would get up. I assumed he went fishing since his clubs were still in the closet."

"You two have a boat, correct?" The sheriff tried to mimic David's body language, but it came across as awkward as Mary backed her body away.

"Yes, docked at the import."

"We will check and see if it is still there. That may give us some answers," the sheriff said.

"What kind of law did your husband practice," David asked, reading her face and body language. She appeared to be in shock, and upset, but not how he might have expected.

"Corporate. Typically dealt with contracts and things like that. He never told me much."

"Anything that might make someone upset?"

"Upset enough to murder him?" She asked. "No. Not that he has ever mentioned. He was going to retire in five years."

"I think we have taken up enough of your time," Tom said as he stood. David followed suit. "If you think of anything, please let us know. And we will keep you up to date on anything we find. Sorry, again, for your loss."

"I am sorry as well," David said giving her a card. "If you need to talk or process any of this, feel free to give me a call."

"Thank you. Both of you."

Once outside the sheriff turned to David. "What was your take?"

"She seemed upset. But she didn't seem entirely surprised."

"That was my read as well."

"So, what do we do now?"

"Check the port and see if these two poor bastards pissed off the same guy. Braden was in business and Chanceler did corporate law. That might be our tie."

"Maybe," David agreed. But inside, he knew it was something else. Something he had not quite figured out.

CHAPTER 34

After checking the port Sheriff Tom and David returned to Tom's office. The port had no record of Chanceler taking the boat out any time over the previous forty-eight hours and it had still been tied up at the dock when they arrived.

Tom's phone rang just as they sat at the desk.

"Yes, this is Sheriff Tom."

Muffled speaking came from the other side of the line.

"Okay, thank you." Tom hung up and leaned back in his chair.

"What was that?"

Tom shook his head as if he could not mentally process whatever he had been told. "ME over in Chicago. Chanceler had a blood-thorn rose shoved into his esophagus. After his throat had been slit."

David felt his blood go cold.

"I cannot believe I let you talk me into letting you come along. David is going to have my ass."

"I can be persuasive when I need to be."

Jack and Bella arrived in Chicago almost an hour and a half after leaving Havana. Forty-five minutes longer than it should have taken. Jack snarled, almost to himself, "I forgot how much I hate Chicago traffic."

"This is light," Bella said.

"Is your attitude always so positive?"

"Yes."

"No wonder David likes you so much."

Jack navigated the congested streets of downtown Chicago until he reached the office of the medical examiner.

"What is the plan?" Bella asked, unhooking herself from the seat.

"You stay here," he told her exiting the car. "David would be pissed enough knowing I brought you. Plus," he said checking to make sure he was not about to be run over. "You have to be credentialed to go inside."

Bella watched Jack jog across the two-lane road and into the grey box. It looked dismal and depressing, she thought. She imagined how lonely of a place it must be, a sad place for one to end up.

As she let her thoughts ponder the darkness inside the building, she spotted a man walking down Harrison Street, where the office was located. He was heading west, and he turned his head for just a moment. Bella recognized him. It was Mr. Roads.

Bella opened her door and exited the car, kneeling just behind the hood to make sure he would not see her if he turned around again. When he turned left down Leavitt Street she sprang from her hiding spot and ran across the street. She stopped at the corner and sent Jack a text, letting him know she was following Mr. Roads and she would meet him at the car and fill him in. Her chest was pounding from nervousness.

He was already two blocks ahead of her. She made her way between cars, ducking behind every third one to conceal her location, though she never saw him turn around. She continued her pursuit another couple of blocks until they reached Livingston Field Park.

She had lost sight of him and began walking aimlessly around one of the ball fields, hopeful that she looked inconspicuous, in case he happened by her. She rounded the field and ended up near a patch of trees. She sat on a concrete bench and after a few moments of scanning the park for Mr. Roads, she found herself staring up at the leaves. They swayed rhythmically in a soft breeze with the grace of a ballet dancer.

"Bella," a harsh voice said from behind her, "I am surprised to see you here."

Bella stood and turned to find Mr. Roads standing behind her. He was looking at her quizzically, and then provocatively as if undressing her with his eyes. "Oh, Mr. Roads," she felt her throat tighten. "I like to come up here sometimes and imagine what it would be like to live in such a wonderful city."

Mr. Roads nodded, but his eyes seemed to say he did not quite believe her. "Most people who do that stay by the lake or in the shopping district."

"I work on the lake and don't make enough to shop."

This made him smile, and his doubtfulness seemed to fade. "That is a fair point, I suppose." He took a step toward her and she forced herself to stay. "I have a meeting in an hour. Why don't you let me treat you to dinner tonight?"

"I wish I could," she said as she brushed a stray hair from her face. "But I have to work tonight."

"I'll call Brent and tell him you can't make it."

"Oh, I wouldn't want to put them out like that. It's Friday and that is the busiest night of the week."

She could tell from his change in expression he was a man who did not like to hear no. She quickly tried to change the subject. "What is your meeting about? Buying a new company?"

He smiled smugly, "No, discussing new delivery times into the port."

"Well, if you get back before it's too late, come by the diner. Desert will be on me."

"I like the sound of that," he said. "I better get going." He turned his back on her and walked away. Bella took a deep breath and her lungs burned. She sprinted back towards her car to meet Jack.

"What the hell were you thinking?" He shouted when she turned the corner. "You trying to get us both killed?"

"I had a feeling."

"And? Did he confess to you from your delightful charm?" His tone was exaggerated and mocking.

"No, but he said he had a meeting about changing delivery times at the port."

"What is that supposed to mean to me? How is that helpful to what we are trying to find out?"

"You can be kind of a jerk," she said. "Did you know that?"

"I've heard it a time or two."

"Well, they deliver necessities at the same time every week. They have for years."

"And?" His tone did not hide his frustration.

"So, he must be talking about another delivery that comes in. When no one else is at the port. David said he saw boats coming in and making deliveries during off-hours."

Jack considered this for a moment, "Or maybe the delivery is not to Havana. Maybe the delivery is coming to Chicago."

CHAPTER 35

David entered the house at a quarter past four. Bella was in a pair of tight jeans and a white blouse; he wanted nothing more than to wrap her in his arms. He met her at the kitchen island where she had a glass of wine waiting on him, Jack was at the opposite end of the island drinking Jack Daniels.

"How was day two of being a cop?" Jack asked.

"Honestly, most of the time we sit in his office. We have talked to Chanceler's wife and he told me his body had been found with a blood-thorn rose in it." David swallowed hard as the image of a rose being stuffed down the deceased man's throat re-entered his mind. "But most of the time we throw around hypotheticals, then he sends his men out to do the investigating."

"Sounds like he is intentionally keeping you out of it," Bella said. "Feeding you just enough to think he is letting you in."

"My thoughts exactly." David took a sip of the wine. "What about you," He asked Jack.

"Sounds like most of policing. The higherups give the orders and everyone else carries them out. Or he could be keeping you in the dark," Jack balanced his hands to either side of his body as if weighing the possibilities. "I drove up to Chicago," he said, leaving Bella out of it intentionally. "The ME mentioned the rose. But she also mentioned something else interesting."

"What was that?"

"That he died from a drug overdose. Something they haven't seen much of, but resembles heroin. He was mutilated up post-mortem."

"Blood Thorn?"

"I had our ME send her some labs for comparison. But I think so."

"So, we have two dead men, murdered. One found in a patch of blood-thorn bushes and one with a rose shoved down his throat. This new drug might be what all of this is about."

"Do you think they were selling it?" Bella asked.

"I doubt it. I mean they made plenty of money on their own. It isn't like they needed drug money."

"Sometimes the rich get bored," Jack offered.

Bella looked at her watch. "I have to get to the diner. I will be back around midnight."

"Okay," David said. He leaned in and kissed her. "Maybe I'll come by and grab some dinner."

"No, it is a busy night. I won't have time to chat." Bella shot Jack an eye, remembering their conversation and the plan they had thought of to try and get more information from Mr. Roads. Bella hated lying and she could feel her stomach knotting up from the act as if she had swallowed a razor and it was cutting her from the inside out.

"Okay," David said. He could tell she was hiding something. He had seen it plenty in his practice. People who had more to say but did not know how.

When Bella left David poured his own bourbon and downed it in a single swallow. "What do we do now? If Sheriff Tom is keeping me out of the investigation, I am just wasting time."

"What about the Ringworm guy?"

"Deputy Ringwall, though he is about as friendly as a ringworm." David shrugged, showing some defeat. "The sheriff says he works and goes home. Doesn't have much of a personal life."

"Do you believe him?"

"I checked the logbook—every deputy has to sign out when they leave Havana—and he hasn't left in months."

Jack cocked his head to the side, "Not that he reported anyway."

"They don't make much money. He could be hungry for some extra cash," David admitted.

"Well, I ran his financials. Nothing jumps out. He is as frugal as he is boring."

"I guess that marks him off the list."

Jack shook his head and let out a long sigh of doubt. "Not necessarily. There are as many ways to hide money as there are to skin a cat. I just need more evidence before I can go digging for them."

"Kind of leaves us between a rock and a hard place, doesn't it?"

"When you went into Caroline and Braden's house, you said you found a secret compartment?"

"Yes."

"And did the sheriff's men find anything when they went back."

"He said no but at this point, I can't be sure that is true."

"Well," Jack said finishing another glass. "No offense, but you are not a trained investigator. I am sure there is something you missed there. Even these deputies aren't equipped for a thorough investigation at a crime scene."

"So, what are you suggesting?"

"We go back. Tonight. And I take a look at this place."

David shook his head. "That is too risky. If anyone finds us…"

Jack lifted his hand to crush the comment away. "They won't. I am very good at my job."

Four hours later the sun was low enough to cast deep shadows on the beach. The two men waded in the water as they walked towards the Baker's home, ensuring their prints would be washed away by the tide. They would then cut up through the blood-thorn roses and into the small patch of woods. Two blocks later they would be at the Baker's residence and would be able to sneak in. Hopefully never being seen.

At the house, David pointed to the back door. "That is how I got in last time. I still have the key. I meant to return it, but never did."

"Lucky us." Jack pulled a Glock 17 from his hip and moved the slide back just enough to reveal a speck of copper resting in the chamber.

"Is that necessary?"

"Whoever killed those guys came back here looking for something. Now that Barney Fife and the boys have searched the house, they have no reason to be back. I assume this guy knows that."

"Fair enough."

After Jack holstered his pistol, the two crept up from the wood line and when they were sure no one was on the docks and the street was clear, they ran for the back door. David tried the knob and it was unlocked.

Jack grabbed him by the arm as he prepared to enter. He motioned down to his feet as he was removing his shoes. David did the same and the two placed their shoes behind a pair of beach chairs leaning against the rail to their right.

"What do we do if the Sheriff's department is casing the place? Or does a drive-by?"

"We duck. Plus, we don't usually case a crime scene unless we are pretty sure the perp will be back. And they don't have the manpower to just station someone outside."

Jack removed a tac-light from his front pocket and covered the bulb with his left hand. He flicked the button once and the light shone through his flesh, turning it a mystical peach color revealing his bones and veins. A second click caused the light to flutter rapidly, and the third click turned the light a deep red. Jack removed his left hand from in front of it and then pointed it low to the ground.

"Show me where you found the ledger."

David began walking towards the hall, but when they passed the living room, Jack stopped him. "Did you notice this when you were here?"

David turned and saw Jack pointing the red beam to an overturned chair in the far-left corner. A dark stain was on the back of the seat and it looked sticky. David followed Jack over to it.

"No," David said.

"That's blood." Jack turned his light to a desk that sat beside the chair. One drawer was open and the contents within had been rustled. "They were looking for something. My guess is when they didn't find it, they tried beating it out of him."

"Guess the sheriff really is trying to keep me on a leash."

"Fuck him." Jack began looking through the drawer and then each one below it. After searching the five drawers he returned them to how he had found them.

"What are you looking for?"

"Nothing."

"Nothing?"

"If there were something of use in there, either the cops should have bagged it or the killer would have found it. I was looking for what was missing."

David was impressed. He knew that Jack was a good cop, he knew that Jack loved his work. But he had never seen him in the field. David hated it, but had to admit, he was impressed. In fact, he was proud of his friend. "How could you tell if something isn't there?"

"If it were something of size, there would be an obvious void. If it were something small, like a USB, I wouldn't."

Jack flicked the light back towards the hall they started down. David led him into the office and showed him where the secret compartment had been. Jack knelt and crawled under the desk and began searching the rest of it. Then, he looked behind the desk.

"Found something," he said as he bent over the top of it, careful not to disrupt anything.

"What?" David's heart began to pound.

"Another book." Jack brought the black leather-bound book up and opened it. It was similar to the ledger David had found, but the entries were different. "It looks like dates and times."

David peered over Jack's shoulder. "It stops the week they went missing." David scanned the lines. "Wait."

David took the book into his own hands and flipped the pages. "All of these dates are four days apart. All the times are the same."

"So?"

"These times match up to when I saw the men unloading boats on the dock. They were only a day apart, but the times are the same."

Jack thought back to what Bella had said. Mr. Roads was changing delivery schedules. Had the first step been to change the frequency?

"I need to tell you something," Jack said as he grabbed the ledger and tucked it into his front pocket.

"What?"

"Let's go get a drink first. We will both need it."

The two turned to leave, David's heart racing, fearing what Jack was going to tell him. "I would rather hear this now."

"Over a drink." He began walking again. "Oh, and remember. I can kick your ass," he reminded David.

CHAPTER 36

"I told her you would be pissed."

David leaned back in the chair. "It was dangerous, Jack. I am not even qualified to be involved with all of this. I do not want her getting into harm's way."

"That's what I told her. She is hard-headed."

"She is confident."

"Same difference," Jack took a shot of the bourbon and filled his glass again.

"Anyway, what about this ledger? They must mean something. And why is the sheriff keeping me at arm's length about it all?"

"Well, the second part of that question is easy," Jack said. "You are an outsider. Not a cop. Not a part of Havana. He is afraid that you will either leak the information and this little paradise will be swarmed with state cops, or that the media will find out."

"When did you become such an expert on the human condition?" David poured himself a glass of wine, twirled the glass gently, and took a sip.

"Since my best friend became a therapist and psychoanalyzed me all the damn time." After finishing his second shot, Jack looked at David. His eyes were serious. Inquisitive. "Speaking of which, why are you so invested in all of this?"

"What do you mean? Why am I invested in figuring out what happened to my client?"

Jack shook his head, "That isn't what this is, and you know it. You reported her missing. That was all you had to do. Why did you come to Havana? Why did you break into their house? Why are you involved in the murder investigation of her husband? Why?"

David felt his heart thump, the sensation brought with it a moment where David felt he might pass out. "Because she is my client."

Jack leaned in, "Bull shit, David. I know you and I know you would not risk your reputation and your career just because she is a client. Since day one you have gone against every ethical code you have. Did you sleep with her?"

David's eyes began to burn, he felt them moisten as the words rose in his throat and exited his mouth. "Because of Alice," he admitted to himself as much as to Jack.

Jack let out a soft sigh, having gotten his answer. It was the answer he expected, not the answer hc hoped for. "That was fifteen years ago, David. There was nothing you could do, man. You have to let it go."

"She called me, Jack. I could have picked her up. I could have not talked to her and maybe she would be less distracted. How could you say there was nothing I could have done?"

"How many clients do you tell that the 'what-if game' is useless? What if doesn't mean shit. Only what is. You were fifty miles away at school. You were doing what you were supposed to be doing."

"She died because of me."

"She died because some dick head decided to get plastered and drive home. And because you think you could have saved her and failed; you are trying to save Caroline. This is not your responsibility either, Dave."

David shook his head, "Even if you are right, even if there is nothing I could have done to change what happened to Alice, I must live with the fact that I didn't even try. I have a chance to try now. Even if this goes south and she is already dead, at least I know I tried. I have to see this through, Jack. Or I will not be able to forgive myself."

Jack looked at his friend and he understood. He had never lost someone he loved. Not the way David loved Alice. He had lost partners and friends and all in situations where he believed he could have saved them. But it was not the same. The loss was part of his job description, but it was not for David.

And he knew that this may be both of their chances at redemption.

"Okay, brother. We will find her. One way or another we will find her." Jack poured himself a third shot and opened the ledger. "Then maybe we will both be able to sleep at night."

⚜

Mr. Roads entered the café just after eight. Brent had just finished another round of plates for Bella when she noticed him take his unofficial place at the counter. She noticed Mr. Roads nod to Brent, which was not unusual, but it felt different.

"Evening, Mr. Roads. I will be right with you." Bella delivered the plates to their destined table and as the men and women rhythmically chimed their forks into the glass plates, she put a menu down on the counter.

"I will just take the special," he said. "And why don't you grab some coffee and go on break? Sit with me for a bit."

"Oh, I wish I could, but it is so busy tonight."

"Brent," Mr. Roads shouted with a tilt of his head in Bella's direction. Brent looked to her, then to Mr. Roads, and gave a simple nod.

Brent called for the other waitress to grab the next round of plates. Bella knew that her tables

244

would be fine for at least ten minutes. Despite the diner being at full capacity, it was only two tables and three counter spots for her. All of them had their food and full drinks. So, she grabbed herself a coffee cup, filled it to the brim, and sat down.

CHAPTER 37

David woke the next morning with a slight headache. Yet, felt a cathartic relief he had not expected. David knew the dangers of holding in grief and not processing trauma, and yet, he had allowed his own to build over the years. Talking to Jack, unexpectedly, helped. He had not discussed his guilt over Alice since the accident. David felt free, for the first time, in a very long time.

He and Jack continued drinking and had been up until the early morning hours sipping liquor and trying to decipher the ledgers. The best they could come up with was that the first ledger David found were dates of purchase or pick up and the initials were buyers or dealers. There were six different initials used throughout the entire ledger. More interestingly, David thought, was that the dates in the first book were two to three days before the dates in the second. Jack concluded that the second ledger kept track of the arrivals or departures of the boats.

Also, during their evening of drinking David and Jack came up with a plan. David was going to press Sheriff Tom about leaving him out of the investigation as well as ask about the boats he saw. This, according to Jack, would let them know if the sheriff was being cautious of outsiders, or if he had something deeper to hide. Either way, they would know where they stood with the Havana Sheriff's Department and whether they would be better off on their own.

⁂

The sheriff was in his office drinking from his mug, as David expected he would be. A pile of papers in front of him seemed to never shrink despite how many pages he removed from the top. David sat across from him and the sheriff waved a hand in the air to someone outside of the office. A second later, David had his cup of coffee. He took one sip and then started the conversation.

"So, I have a question," David said in a low voice. Afraid that his words would travel to the ears of other deputies and he would become a sacrifice to the small pack of feral beasts. A gift from their leader.

"What's that?"

"I have this hunch that you are intentionally keeping me on the outside with all of this. Letting me know just enough to feel like I am part of the investigation, but not enough to help. I want to know why."

David watched the sheriff as he shifted in his seat. His body fluctuated from left to right causing the chair to squeal with each move. David could tell what the sheriff was thinking, but he could not tell if the man was upset or surprised.

"You are right, Mr. Thorne. I have been keeping you on the outside."

"What is the reason?" David asked as he leaned in closer.

"Because you are an outsider," he said simply. "You show up to Havana and all of the sudden, a town with zero crime, winds up with two bodies."

"Do you suspect me?"

"No. But I cannot rule anything out. Maybe you had nothing to do with this, but maybe a pissed-off client followed you here to take revenge. Or maybe you go blabbing everything to an outside agency. Neither scenario is particularly good."

Good for who, David wondered. For Havana? For his department? "It seems to me that whoever is behind this targeted those two men for a specific reason. Something that ties *them* together. I am an easy man to find, if someone wanted to hurt me, they would have."

"That still doesn't make me certain you won't feed any of this to an outside agency. We don't want the extra bull shit here." The sheriff's face grew stern.

"Again, if that were my intention, it would have happened. My only interest is to make sure Caroline is safe and Braden's killer is brought to justice."

The sheriff seemed to consider his words for a long time. Rocking slightly in his chair. "Okay," he said with a heavy exhale. It was as if the breath signified his releasing information. "This does not leave the room, is that clear?"

"Crystal."

"We think someone from this department was behind both murders." He shook his head as if correcting his thoughts. "Well, I do."

"Who?"

As the sheriff's mouth opened there was a knock on the door. Deputy Ringwall walked in and the sheriff's eyes narrowed.

⚘

"He is getting too close," the man said to the figure within the shadows. He pulled his father's revolver from the desk, spun the cylinder, and then jammed the loaded pistol into his pocket.

The figure groaned acknowledging the man's words.

"He knows more than he will admit. He and his little bitch are two loose ends we cannot have dangling around."

The figure let out a chuckle which made even the man's blood cool. He was no stranger to violence and the grotesque nature that came with doing business. But the figure seemed to relish in the gore. He seemed to be turned on by the idea of harming. For the man, it was simply standard practice for his line of work, both legal and illegal. But that was not the case for the silhouette before him.

"We will take care of them both. All our loose ends will be severed tonight." The man felt the firmness of the firearm in his pocket. He knew that if they did not clean up now, everything he had built would be ruined.

CHAPTER 38

David returned home a little after three. Bella walked in a minute later carrying a bag of sandwiches and some chips. She set them on the counter as David poured lemonade from a pitcher. He gave a cup to Bella, then Jack, and then one to himself.

"How did your talk with Roads go last night?" David asked.

Bella's face showed her shock that David knew she was going to be talking with Mr. Roads. "We had a heart-to-heart last night," Jack said, "He knows everything."

"I wanted to keep you safe. But I know you are more than capable of taking care of yourself," David told her.

With a sense of relief, she answered David's original question. "Weird."

"How so?" Jack spat out lettuce and a bit of tomato as he spoke.

Bella waited until she swallowed her bite to speak. "He said someone was trying to screw him and he was going to make them pay."

Jack slammed a fist on the counter and smiled triumphantly. "I told you he had something to do with this!"

David tossed a chip in his mouth. "I did not get that from what she said. He runs a big business empire. He could have been talking about anything."

"Really, David? We have two dead bodies and you don't think that comment means anything?"

"It might. But it might not. Besides, Sheriff Tom said the reason I was kept on the outside was that he didn't know if he could trust me. But he thinks Deputy Ringwall has something to do with it. Said that Ringwall has a short fuse—which I can attest to—and that he recently made some big purchases that his salary does not cover. The department is doing an internal investigation."

"Hopefully they are better at solving that case than they are at solving murders," Bella said.

"That makes sense," Jack agreed. "You never share sensitive information with an outsider. You don't know their angle and they could fuck you in the end."

"Pretty much what he said."

"Well, if the ledger really is about the new drug hitting the streets, they may both be in on it. I had a friend of mine in computer crimes do some homework. He said that Roads has no money to his name. About a month ago his accounts went dry. A week before Caroline and Braden went missing Roads was cited for assault."

"Don't you need a warrant for his financial information?"

"First off, mister, are you questioning me about ethics?"

David felt his face flush.

"Secondly, I am not officially investigating anything. If that time comes, I will pass this information on to Chicago and the local PD here—anonymously, of course—and they can get a warrant."

"Fair enough. So, who did Roads assault?"

"Guess."

"Braden?"

"Bingo!"

"That can't be a coincidence," Bella pointed out.

"That's what I thought. But I was proven right when two days later Chanceler Wells' wife called to report a car sitting outside of their Chicago house. It matches the description of Roads to a 'T.' He was gone by the time police arrived but I would bet it was him. Now, less than three weeks after, both men wind up dead? What are the odds they would both have trouble with Roads?"

David thought for a moment, "Roads is a narcissist. There is no doubt about that. But I do not think he killed them. He is too smart. He built a multi-billion-dollar empire. A man like that doesn't go around killing people over drug deals. Which is another thing, why would a man like that need to get into the drug game?"

Jack nodded as if he had already considered this, which David knew, he had. But Bella answered for him.

"Maybe that is where Ringwall comes in. Mr. Roads hired him to kill Braden and Chanceler, he is a cop and would know how to cover it up. He also made those purchases the sheriff mentioned, so the money came from somewhere. And he thinks he is invincible, above the law. This is like a game to him, he does it because he can."

Jack nodded and pointed his thumb at Bella as if confirming she had just read his mind.

"There is another possibility," David said. "A third person, we haven't identified is setting them both up to look guilty."

"What would be the motive," Jack insisted.

"Mr. Roads is an asshole. What better motive is there than that? Deputy Ringwall is a nobody. He is expendable."

"Fine," Jack said swallowing the last bite of his sandwich whole. "I'll play. Let's pretend there is a third party. Who would have it out for two men who have nothing in common and who are two worlds apart?"

"And also have it out for Chanceler and the Bakers?" Bella reminded them.

"That's a good question," David conceded.

Bella looked at her watch, "I have to get back to the diner for the dinner rush. A girl called in."

"Come back tonight," David asked hopefully.

"Of course," she said with a smile before rounding the counter and kissing him gently.

"That is disgusting. You gonna finish this." Jack said before picking up the last half of Bella's sandwich and taking a bite.

"No, it is all yours."

"Thanks."

David walked Bella to the door and kissed her once more, this time without Jack's commentary.

He returned to the kitchen and finished his lemonade.

"So, what is our next move?"

"We need to figure out what all four had in common. Probably the drugs." David said. "If we can figure out who the fifth member is, if there is a fifth, then we know who set all of this in motion."

"And if there isn't a fifth?"

"Then I will admit it was Roads."

"How do you suppose we do this? Whoever is behind this is going to be on edge now. They seem like they are scrambling. Plus, I am not supposed to be here and you are already under a microscope."

"There should be a shipment coming in tonight. At least according to the past ledgers."

"Roads said he was working to get that switched up."

"Well, maybe he didn't. And that is also assuming he is the killer. If not, then the shipment should be on time. And whoever is behind all of this will be there to see it arrive."

"I need more than just my Glock then. Can you go grab my duffle bag from my room?"

"Why can't you?"

"Because I am the guest."

David returned two minutes later with a black duffle bag and set it on the kitchen island. Jack opened it and pulled out a Smith & Wesson M&P AR-15. The rifle already had a magazine in it, a fancy optic on top of the firearm, and a sling made from some sort of cord.

"Paracord," Jack said when David felt it. "It is the Swiss Army Knife of cordage."

Then he pulled out a smaller version of the Glock 17 he carried on his hip. He said it was a Glock 42. "Six rounds of .380. Not a main firearm, but can save your ass if you need it to."

"This seems like an awful lot of firepower."

"I have met a lot of drug dealers in my day. With two dead bodies already on the slab, these guys are not any less violent than the ones outside the gate. If shit gets hairy, we will need every bit of it." Jack slid the smaller Glock across the island to David and then put a small pocket holster next to it.

"No thanks," David said sliding it back in Jack's direction.

"This isn't a debate, Dave. I got your six, but as I said, if it goes south you need to be able to protect yourself."

"With six shots?"

Jack pointed to the holster which held two additional magazines. "What time will the boats be here?"

"Around midnight. They spend about an hour at the dock and then head off."

"We need to get confirmation that someone other than Roads—or even Roads—is receiving the shipment and that drugs are being delivered."

"How will we know if they are drugs?"

Jack shook his head. "No way safe. We will have to confirm it ourselves. Either by following them if they move it somewhere or by going into the dock house to inspect it when they leave. If they are moving a large load, they will have to store it somewhere for at least a day or two."

CHAPTER 39

Bella left the diner just after 10 p.m. The streets were dark and the immense heat, which had plagued Havana and the rest of northern Indiana for most of the month, had begun to subside to a cool crisp wind. She welcomed it as the breeze wisped at the sweat on her brow. She took in a deep breath from the summer night when a voice startled her, causing her to turn with her fists clenched ready to attack.

"Did I scare you?" She looked up at the voice to see Mr. Roads standing just inches from her. She wondered how she had not heard him approaching. Bella looked around but did not see his cart. She then looked over to the police station, but no one was outside.

"No," she lied, "Just had my mind busy on other things."

"You know my offer still stands." He bent down and handed her the keys she had been struggling to grasp with her shaking fingers.

"I appreciate that, Mr. Roads. But as I said, I am seeing someone."

"You know," he said lowering his voice and taking another uncomfortable step into her personal space. "Not many people tell me no and don't regret it."

Suddenly, a new voice cut the tension. But it startled her more than Mr. Roads'. "Roads, leave the girl alone."

"What do you want?" Roads' body went tense and he resembled a stray dog caught in the corner ready to fight for an escape. Roads lost all his strength and, at that moment, appeared small and weak. Bella turned to face the man speaking.

He held a revolver in one hand pointing it directly between her and Mr. Roads. His hand was steady and the hammer had been pulled back, ready to fire. She recognized the man and the figure behind him.

"Let's go for a ride," the man said.

Mr. Roads began yelling at the man, but she could not process the words being thrown around. Then she felt a sharp sting in her neck and everything went dark.

※

David was about to reach for the doorknob when a bang came from the other side of the door. Then another. And another. He turned and shot Jack a look. Jack ducked behind a pillar to David's right, which concealed Jack as long as whoever was out there did not come in and walk by it.

David opened the door on Jack's signal.

"Dr. Neil," David said.

"How ya doin' buddy?" Dr. Neil asked.

"Good, just about to take a walk."

Dr. Neil nodded his head but his face showed a sign of doubt. "Good, I will go with you."

"Oh, no," David said in a tone as to insist he did not want to burden the elder gentleman.

"I insist. I think we should go for a walk. Now."

David noted Dr. Neil's face was dark and stern. It was not the same fun-loving face David had come to know. He also noticed Dr. Neil reaching into his pocket.

Jack unholstered his Glock and raised it to the ready. He could see the reflection of the two men in a small picture frame mirror hanging on the wall behind David. He did not like what he was seeing.

"You know, on second thought," David began. He started to shift his body so that he could use his weight to force the door shut if he needed. "I do not feel great. I might sit down for a while. I will call you if I change my mind."

"David, you need to come with me." His face was sullen and it scared David.

"What is going on, Dr. Neil?"

Dr. Neil leaned in and in a low quaking whisper said, "there is someone in your house."

CHAPTER 40

After David introduced Dr. Neil to Jack, the two men explained to Dr. Neil what they suspected Mr. Roads of and how the sheriff had been keeping David in the dark about the investigations, Dr. Neil leaned back and shook his head. It was as if he were trying to make the pieces fit in his mind to make sense.

"You know," Dr. Neil said, "it doesn't surprise me the sheriff wouldn't be very forthcoming."

"Why is that?" Jack asked, checking his watch to make sure they still had time to get to the docks.

"Because if he thinks Mr. Roads is behind anything like what you say, he would want to make him burn."

"Why would he have such animosity towards him?"

"Well," Dr. Neil said, "all of this used to belong to the sheriff's family. He wanted to donate a portion of it to the state to make it a park. Somehow Roads snaked his way in and bought up ninety percent of his family plot. Said he was doing a service by letting Tom stay on as sheriff. Allowing him to protect his family's heritage."

"That does not make sense. How could he just come in a buy up the property? Especially if Sheriff Tom was not selling it?"

Dr. Neil shook his head, "I do not know. All I know is that a man that rich and connected can do almost anything he wants."

⁂

Bella's head was throbbing. Her stomach felt like a lead weight had been placed inside of her and threatened to exit upward. She swallowed hard and opened her eyes, which fought her every inch of the way. Even they felt heavy.

She could not tell where she was, the room was dark and smelled of mildew. It was cold, despite the temperature being in the upper eighties that night. Some sort of basement?

She heard two men arguing and forced her eyes to follow the sound of the voices. A few feet to her right stood the silhouette of a man, in front of him, Mr. Roads.

"Fuck you! Do you know who you are fucking with?" Mr. Roads' anger was evident as he stood screaming at the man who pointed his hand into the face of Roads.

"I have waited a long time for this, Roads."

Bella suddenly realized the man was not pointing just his hand into Mr. Roads' face. It was a gun.

"I built paradise and this is how you repay me? You ungrateful fuck."

"Mr. Roads, not a day has gone by that I have not dreamed of putting a bullet in your head. But then I would think, that is too easy. It does not provide the suffering you deserve. You deserve a long agonizing death. You deserve to watch helplessly as everything you love burns to the fucking ground."

Mr. Roads must have noticed a change in the man's face because his boisterous yells lowered to a tone ready to negotiate. "What do you want from me? I am your brother for Christ's sake."

The man shook his head. "I told you what I want, Mr. Roads. And it's funny how that worked out, isn't it?"

"What's that," Mr. Roads' voice shook, less sure and less angry than it had been.

"The same gun I used to kill dad I am using to kill you."

Bella shrieked at the loud bang. The dark room was suddenly lit by a magnificent yellow hue that disappeared just as rapidly as it had come. She saw Mr. Roads' head shoot back viciously, a ball of red liquid spraying from behind his head. Then, his

264

head lowered slowly, a small red dot in the center of his forehead. He looked at the man before him, wondering how he dared to do such a thing.

Then his body collapsed, folding on top of itself like a towel discarded in the corner by an unconcerned owner.

The man turned from the body towards Bella. "I am so glad you are awake. You won't want to miss this."

"I don't know anything! I didn't see anything! Just let me go!"

"I need you."

"Why?"

"Because you are the key to David Thorne."

Bella's eyes widened and her voice became trapped in her throat. A ball of pain grew suddenly in her esophagus which made it hard to breathe.

"Now," the man said, "you two enjoy some quiet time. It is about to get very, very messy around here." He nodded his head to the left and Bella's eyes followed.

Caroline Baker was tied to a pipe. She was conscious, but only barely. Bruises lined her face and deep gashes arched across the flesh of her arms. A bottle of dirty water half drank, sat beside her, just outside of her reach.

CHAPTER 41

The house phone rang which startled the three men.

"Who has this number?"

"No one that would be calling me," David said. He decided to let it ring, assuming it was a wrong number or a telemarketer.

"You should pick it up," Jack said.

"Why?"

"Call it a cop's hunch."

David huffed as if Jack's suggestion were some sort of disturbance to his being. "Hello?" David said.

"Mr. Thorne," the voice was gravelly. He did not recognize it, but he knew that it was not a telemarketer. He looked to Jack, eyes wide, nodding to confirm the gut instinct Jack had.

"Who is this?"

"That is no concern of yours. But what is, is who we have keeping us company tonight."

David's heart fell hard into his stomach, almost causing him to collapse. "Don't you touch her! If you want me, fine, I will come to wherever you want me to. But you let her go!"

"That is not how this game goes. There is an old cabin in the woods near the demolished shack. Go into the basement."

"How do I know you won't just shoot me when I get there?"

"You don't," the voice said. "But if you're not there in fourteen minutes, I promise I will shoot your little bitch." The line went silent.

"How long does it take to get to the old shack on the west end of the beach from here?"

"In my cart?" Dr. Neil asked for the sake of asking. "Three, maybe four minutes."

"What did they say?" Jack asked.

"They have Bella."

"Fuck!"

"Wait," Dr. Neil said in shock, standing so quickly from his seat that he almost fell. "Who?"

"I don't know. But I have to be inside the old cabin by the dock in thirteen minutes or they kill her. So, we have seven minutes to come up with a plan."

"I'm going too," Dr. Neil said.

"No, it is too dangerous. I don't want to get you involved. Call the state police and tell them where I am."

"To hell with that, son. I think of Bella as a daughter. No way am I letting you two handle this alone. Besides, retirement has been a boring drag."

"So, what is the plan?" David asked, directing the question to Jack.

"Here is what we will do," he said.

CHAPTER 42

David arrived at the cabin with two and a half minutes to spare. He went inside and began shouting about his arrival, to ensure whoever was waiting for him knew he had arrived. It was nothing more than an attempt to keep Bella alive. He would not lose her, too.

The cabin reeked of mold, and the floor beneath him bowed with each step. Cobwebs decorated the corners of the ceiling and the furniture which remained were each covered by sheets and a decade or more worth of dust. At first, David wondered how such a decrepit piece of structure could be left standing in Havana. Then, he realized, it belonged there.

David scanned the room, but the darkness along the wooden walls grew the further away he looked. He saw only two doors in the room he was in and he began walking briskly toward the one to the right. When he reached the door, he tugged it open and saw the stairs. A dim yellow hue lit the bottom of the stairs.

He flexed his calf to feel the Glock 42 holstered to his ankle. Jack had made sure the chamber was hot, a term Jack used and David did not

269

like. Then he flexed his chest where they had strapped a makeshift wire to him. In reality, it was Dr. Neil's cell phone, on call to Jack's cell, in case they wanted David's.

He began his descent, each step screaming under his weight.

§

"He isn't saying anything," Dr. Neil said. He had a pair of wired earphones stuffed into his ears. Jack was amazed they still made wired anything.

"If he uses the code, we will be ready to roll. Do you remember your part?"

"Lay low and call the police if shit hits the fan."

"Exactly." Jack scanned the surrounding area of the cabin with his scope to make sure there was no movement. He saw none. He rose to his knees ready to advance. Dr. Neil said there should be a window leading to the basement which led to a small furnace room. If he could get in, Jack would be able to reach David in a matter of milliseconds if need be.

Jack crept through the shadows, concealing himself in the line of trees which separated the house from the openness beyond. Dr. Neil had vanished in the darkness which brought Jack minor relief. At least no one would see him there, which meant if everything went to hell, someone would be able to call in backup.

Jack spotted a figure standing near the back entrance of the house. An orange bulb lit and then dimmed at the face. Jack caught the faint hint of tobacco in the air. The figure would be distracted as they smoked, but they were twenty yards away. Jack ran scenarios through his mind, but with the distance between them, none played out well for Jack.

He crouched behind a bush, the sight of his weapon trained on the centermost point of the figure's chest. His finger rested gently on the trigger, calm and poised. He held just enough pressure to feel the trigger give slightly, but not enough to fire the round in the chamber. If the figure noticed him, they would be dead before they could yell for anyone.

The figure tossed the cigarette down and stomped on it with a heavy foot. Then the figure turned and rounded the house heading for the front. Once out of sight, Jack continued his slow creep toward his entry point. Once there, Jack sat silently for a moment, listening for the figure. He heard only the sounds of the summer night and once confident the figure had entered the house, he pulled at the handle of the window.

The old rusted latches squealed in protest. To Jack, it sounded as though a siren broke the dead silence of the night. He stopped to listen again but heard nothing. Satisfied he had not betrayed his location nor his intentions, he slid through the gap between the window and the dirt and into the dark room of the cellar.

⁂

Two steps from the bottom David heard the front door open from above. He stopped and for a moment thought about going back up. Maybe Jack or Dr. Neil had seen something and were coming to warn him. Or, someone was coming to ambush him. The light on the other side of the wall to his right seemed much safer and assuring than the prospect of whoever had just come into the house.

David descended the final two steps and turned into the open cellar. Laying in the center of the floor was the body of a man, a pool of blood flooded the floor beneath his head. The man's face was turned away from him, but the pristine Gucci suit was familiar. It was Mr. Roads.

Then David saw Bella, her eyes wide and her body trembling. She seemed to scream for him but no sound came from her. She had been bound to an old wooden chair that, had she so desired, she could have easily broken free from. Then David noticed something to her left. His brain hardly related to what his eyes were seeing. Caroline chained to a pipe running from the wall. Her face was bloodied. She was not moving. He was not sure she was even breathing.

His eyes broke free from the sight when he heard the voice. "Nice of you to join us, Mr. Throne."

CHAPTER 43

"You know, killing you is going to be a real shame," his voice empty and stern, "Bella too. I always liked her. I liked you, too, David. But you just would not leave it alone!"

David stared at him unable to comprehend what was happening. He looked over to Bella trying desperately to tell her it would be all right, but he felt his eyes in their widened state and was unsure if she could read them as he hoped. He turned his attention back to the man pointing a gun to his forehead. A man he had questioned but hoped was innocent in all of this.

"You killed your own brother?"

Tom's face showed how impressed he was. "Smart man. How did you know he was my brother?"

"I remembered Roads telling me about his brother, but he said he did not talk to him. I heard that Roads had blocked you from donating this land to the state. But that didn't make sense. How can someone block you from donating your own land? Then it hit me. He was your brother and would not sign off on it. He wanted to profit from the land. It also explains why you two stopped talking. You must have been furious."

"Very impressive," Tom said mimicking a gentle clap. "So, you know why I killed my brother. Do you know why I killed my dad?"

"I don't think it matters," David said, "I am sure you had your reasons." David wanted Tom to know he was not there to judge him. He also wanted him to know he was not expecting him to clarify his reasons because they were likely justified. At least to Tom.

"I can understand why you would want to get revenge. But what I don't get is why bring everyone else into all of this? Braden? Chanceler Wells?"

"When a friend from the other side of the gates got into smuggling drugs, we decided to cut out the middlemen and become more profitable. Of course, when Roads found out he wanted his grubby paws in the mix. It was perfect." A smile crept onto his face showing a sadistic pleasure that unsettled David.

"I could bury him with this. But in the end," he waived the muzzle of the gun over Roads' body, "I decided to just bury him anyway. And as for Braden, he could not keep his fucking mouth shut. He knew too much and was rapping off at the mouth about it to some guys in Chicago. Chanceler was skimming. You and Bella just got in the way."

"You know people will come looking for me. They know I am here and that I am due back in a

275

couple of days, there will be no getting away from this. Just let Bella and me go. Let Caroline go and you can do whatever you need to do here."

Sheriff Tom smiled, "There is no going back now, David. That is a deep lake out there and there are plenty of places to put a body so it is never found. Get rid of the car and as far as anyone knows you and her ran away together."

David tried to scan the room with his peripheral to see if Jack might have come in. He saw nothing causing sweat to form on his brow. "So, are you going to kill us? Or this friend you told me about?"

"Brent."

"Am I supposed to know him?"

"The cook at the diner. Also, my cousin."

David heard a rapid succession of sounds that he could not at that moment process other than as chaos and reckoning. First was the clicking sound behind his right ear. Then thunderous cracking of wood as it splintered into hundreds of pieces. Then he heard an echoing symphony of small explosions accompanied by bright flashes of light. No pain, though. He heard what sounded like meat being slapped behind him and a shrill cry of a man in pain. Then he heard Bella screaming for him and through the anarchy, he broke free.

276

He ran over to Bella and out of pure instinct dove on top of her splitting the char in half as they landed on the concrete floor. He grabbed her shoulders and pulled her back behind a brick wall. Caroline was still tied to the concrete pillar but the area around her appeared peaceful and calm.

David looked back in the direction of the small blasts and saw a man he presumed to be Brent writhing on the floor. A widening pool of blood beneath him. Then he saw Jack tucked behind a wooden doorframe just behind where David had been standing, a wooden door shattered in front of it. He was shooting at something.

Then David remembered Sheriff Tom. He was moving to his right, small shots coming from his gun. Until there was not.

Jack breached from his position, reloading as he moved but never moving the sight of his gun from Tom. He slapped a new magazine in and slapped the side of his rifle ready to take a shot, which David heard. But he did not see the muzzle flash. Instead, Jack's body twisted violently and crumbled to the ground, a harsh groan passing his lips as he fell.

CHAPTER 44

Sheriff Tom stood from a crouched position, a victorious laugh bellowing from his stomach as he approached Jack, his aim holding steady. David pulled the .38 from the holster Jack had attached to his ankle, "It is hot. Aim and fire," Jack had told him.

David knew he had six shots, hoping that even if he missed, it would give Jack enough time to come to and get behind something. David fired his first shot. The recoil rushed from his hand up into his elbow. A thousand bells began sounding in his ears and all other sounds fell away.

Sheriff Tom ducked and a puff of dust blasted free from the stone wall behind him. He turned towards David and fired three shots in rapid succession. All three were high of David. He felt the dust falling onto his scalp. David returned two more shots, the second of which found its target.

Sheriff Tom's beige shirt quickly turned crimson and a look of fear cloaked his face. He backed up to the wall and slid down. At the bottom, the gun fell free from his hand and his body went limp.

David grabbed Bella. "Are you okay?"

"Yes," she managed to say.

278

David helped her to her feet and broke the duct tape free from her wrists. They both sprinted to Jack, who was still motionless. David grabbed his friend and pulled him into his arms, immediately noticing the blood on his left hand as he did.

"Jack!" He shook his friend. "Jack!"

"Oh my god, David... Is he..."

"Fuck, man. Not so rough, I've been shot."

David's emotions broke the dam built by adrenaline and confusion. He both laughed and cried. "You aren't supposed to get shot, asshole."

Jack sat up and looked down at his right arm. "Just a graze." He looked past Bella and saw Sheriff Tom. "How many shots did it take?"

"Three shots. Maybe four? Or five? I only got one. I think."

Now Jack was chuckling. "Not too bad, buddy." David and Bella stood, each reaching a hand out to help Jack up. Then, without warning, Jack pulled a pistol from his side and fired three shots beyond David and Bella. They both ducked instinctively.

When the echoes of the gunfire silenced, they both looked in the direction Jack had fired. Sheriff Tom was now kneeling clutching his chest with one hand as his gun fell from the other. Then he collapsed, a final breath escaping his body as he did.

They stood there in silence for a moment, then the silence was broken by the sound of approaching sirens.

David did not notice how much time had passed between hearing the sirens and the cascade of screaming voices telling them to get down and to drop their weapons. David and Bella had just freed Caroline, noticing for the first time just how tortured she appeared, when he was roughly pulled from her.

Then he heard Dr. Neil from somewhere behind him screaming, "They are the good guys!"

CHAPTER 45

David put Bella's final bag into the trunk of his car. His body still ached from the showdown two nights before. He was pleasantly surprised by how fast the local police wrapped up their investigation, though they warned David to keep his phone on and not to leave the state until they made it official.

"You are not such a troublemaker, after all, Mr. Throne." Sheriff Ringwall said. His promotion had been suggested by Dr. Neil and the transition had been seamless.

"I could say the same about you. In all honesty, I thought you were behind it all."

Ringwall's face turned a deep red. Not from anger, but embarrassment. "I can be a little brash," he admitted. "But you are welcomed here anytime." He stuck a hand out and shook David's vigorously with a tight grip. He nodded to Dr. Neil and Bella then made his way to his Jeep.

"We sure will miss you around here, young lady." Dr. Neil and his wife each leaned in and hugged Bella. "You too," he said to David shaking his hand. "We haven't had that much excitement in years."

"Who is we?" His wife chimed in, "You left me home in bed and had all of the fun."

"Well, I am just glad to have met the two of you."

"When you see Jack tell him I want some private shooting lessons."

"I will." David looked around at the paradise one last time. "What do you think will happen to Havana now?"

Dr. Neil shrugged. "Plenty of people around here who will jump at the opportunity to take over and run our little oasis. None of them as slimy as Mr. Roads or Sheriff Tom."

"Thank God for that," Bella said.

"You just be sure to come visit us from time to time."

"I will," she said.

Dr. Neil and his wife returned to their cart and drove down the narrow road towards their home, their hands extended from the sides waiving the entire way. When they were out of sight, David pulled Bella close to him.

"Are you sure you want to leave all of this for Indianapolis?"

"I'm not leaving anything for Indianapolis."

"Oh?" He asked.

"I am leaving it for you."

David leaned in and kissed her deeply. "My life is much more boring than what you have in Havana. Especially this past week."

"I doubt that," she said. She kissed him passionately.

1/4/2023

Jack Lawrence   Blood Thorn

ABOUT THE AUTHOR

Jack Lawrence was a therapist in Indiana before becoming an author. He specialized in families and couples and did a lot of work with clients suffering addiction. He currently lives in Indiana with his family and their dog. Blood Thorn is his first novel and the first book in the David Thorne series.

Follow Jack on Social Media:

Facebook

Instagram

Jack Lawrence   Blood Thorn

Manufactured by Amazon.ca
Bolton, ON

35783686R00162